PARKER

The K9 Files, Book 6

Dale Mayer

Books in This Series:

PARKER: THE K9 FILES, BOOK 6
Dale Mayer
Valley Publishing Ltd.

ISBN-13: 978-1-773361-93-2
Print Edition

About This Book

Welcome to the all new K9 Files series reconnecting readers with the unforgettable men from SEALs of Steel in a new series of action packed, page turning romantic suspense that fans have come to expect from USA TODAY Bestselling author Dale Mayer. Pssst... you'll meet other favorite characters from SEALs of Honor and Heroes for Hire too!

Heading back to Iraq was never in Parker's plans ...

But, when his brother is killed in action, he makes the journey to bring his brother back home to his final resting place.

When one of the K9 War Dogs disappears at the military airport in transit, and all attempts to locate him fails, Parker agrees to investigate during the few days he's there.

Sandy is making the same journey as Parker—both of their brothers were killed in the same incident. Both brothers had been the best of friends, but this is the first time she's met Parker. From that initial moment, she realizes something odd is happening in his world. When they find a K9 dog in a rebel stronghold, she's sucked into a much more dangerous trip than one of compassion and grief.

There's a reason why the first investigation didn't turn up anything. ... As Parker rattles cages and shakes up a ring of thieves, the bodies start dropping, one by one.

Sign up to be notified of all Dale's releases here!

http://smarturl.it/dmnewsletter

PROLOGUE

"**A**NOTHER ONE BITES the dust, huh?" Geir sat with his feet up on the boardroom table and smiled at the rest of the team. "I can't believe these K9 guys are all getting hitched, and most of them are keeping the dogs," he said.

"And one murder and an attempted murder have been solved at the same time," Badger said, shaking his head. "That's a doubly awesome job."

"Who'd have thought that the one girlfriend, who worked in dispatch, had overheard the dirty cops discussing the dogfights and their involvement. After that, they couldn't take the chance she'd talk so took her out, then her roommate. They planned to knock off Tanya as well but were just waiting for a better time. In the meantime one of the accountants who worked with Tanya had heard about Tanya's girlfriend's involvement in the dogfighting and didn't want to keep Tanya close, in case she found out anything else—like how the firm was laundering money for the dogfighting rings—so got rid of her too. Doesn't that just make you love people?"

"Not much," Badger said. "It's not what we expected on a mission to save one War Dog. Yet Lucas is responsible for saving more than 160 dogs. And we especially didn't plan the matchmaking success on this op."

Kat came in, a cup of coffee in her hand, and sat down

beside them. "Might not be what we had planned or what you guys had planned," she said, "but it's all good news."

"Says the woman who arranged all our weddings," Geir said, chuckling.

Badger watched the color wash over her cheeks but grabbed her fingers in his and whispered, "Thank God."

She beamed at him. "You guys can hate me until doomsday," she said, "or pretend to, but you know that you're all much better off the way you are now. *Happily married.*"

"Oh, we're not arguing with that," Erick said. "I think we're all happy little pigs in our blankets, but we have more dogs to look after." He spread the files around. "Take a look and see if there's anybody here that we know of to match up with another dog. The commander called to check in the other day. Now we have another success story to tell him. But I'm sure he's wondering what's taking us so long."

"There's no time frame involved," Geir said. He opened the file in front of him and flipped through the pages. "Hell, this one's over in Iraq still."

Badger lifted his head. "Seriously?"

He nodded, his face glum. "The poor dog's probably dead and gone by now."

"Well, that's an interesting state of affairs," Erick said.

Badger looked at him. "Why is that?"

"Because Parker is heading there on a compassionate leave trip. His brother was killed in action. He's planning on escorting his body home. But that doesn't mean, while he's there, he doesn't have a day or two to track down the dog."

"The dog was lost at the military base?" Badger asked.

Geir flipped through the pages. "Yes. And, once it's off the base, it's no longer their problem. To give them their due, everybody did search for the dog. They wondered if it had been stolen. It was decommissioned and due to fly home the next day. Apparently the dog arrived at the airport but disappeared while waiting to be picked up. Its whereabouts after its arrival at the hangar is a mystery. There are discrepancies in the witness statements. They are thinking that maybe somebody close to the airport may have kidnapped the dog."

"Does Commander Cross really want us to go over there and look into this one?" Geir asked, shaking his head. "That's a bit out of the boundaries, isn't it?"

"If it wasn't for Parker heading over there tomorrow, I wouldn't think of looking into this one," Erick said. "If Parker can find the dog, he can bring him home with him as well."

Badger nodded. "Where's Parker now?"

"He's packing, I think. His brother, Jerry, and his crew were taken out by an IED. Jerry's best friend was part of his unit, and Sandy, his best friend's sister, is heading over there with him."

Grins popped up around the table.

Erick nodded. "I know what you're thinking," he said. "She's military too. I think she's a nurse in California. She also asked for special permission to go over there."

"Of course. Bringing family home is important to everyone."

"Do you want to call him?" Badger asked Erick. "You seem to know him the best."

"He's been around for a while, but, yeah, I used to know him in the military too," Erick said. "Unlike the rest of us, he's not missing a body part."

"Unless he's missing his heart," Jager said. "As in pining

for his brother. Maybe it's a good thing this Sandy is going over there too. It's a tough trip for anyone, and it would help to not be alone."

"It's a shit trip no matter who goes with you," Erick said, but he already had his phone out and was dialing.

Geir watched in surprise. "Is he on your contact list?"

Erick nodded. "Yeah, he is."

There was silence for a moment, then Erick was giving his condolences first before adding, "I heard you're heading over to Iraq tomorrow. What base?"

Erick nodded, while they all watched. Then he grinned. He motioned with his hand for the file in front of Geir. "Look. We have an odd request. Commander Cross dropped a dozen files on us filled with K9 agents who served their time and, for one reason or another, have been retired and then lost. We have one that disappeared between the base and the airport in Iraq. We're trying to get him home and settled into a decent life here." Erick was silent as he listened for a short while. Then he said, "Oh, you heard about him?"

He looked around the room. "Great. Do you have any K9 experience?"

Erick frowned and nodded. The others waited. "Okay. If you've got an extra day, and you don't mind taking a look, we would really appreciate being able to tell the commander we have found the dog and have brought him home and have set him up someplace worthy of a War Dog. If that's something you feel you can do, that would be awesome. But we do understand if you can't. Obviously anything to do with your brother comes first. Again our condolences on your loss."

The conversation continued for a few minutes, and Geir and Badger exchanged looks. And then Erick ended the call.

He looked around the table. "Well, he's game. He said he has a couple days over there, and he would look up some friends by the base. And, believe it or not," he added with a note of satisfaction, "he's going to FOB Wild, where the dog went missing."

"*FOB Wild?* That's one of the forward operating bases in the northern Iraqi province of Ninewah, a few miles outside of Tal Afar," Badger said in surprise as he reached for the folder to double-check the location where the dog had gone missing for himself. "That's perfect. Maybe somebody there knows something."

"I hope so," Erick said. "Parker's just leaving the military himself. I think he's done in a couple weeks. Been on medical leave and not going back."

"Understood," Badger said. "Not easy for anybody when losing someone so close to you."

"True enough," Geir said. "Let's just see what happens. Maybe we'll get lucky again."

"You mean, maybe he'll get lucky," Jager said with a grin.

All the men laughed, and Erick nodded. "Luck comes in many forms," he said. "Let's hope he finds one form that suits him."

CHAPTER 1

PARKER CUTTER HOPPED into his borrowed rig and checked the GPS for directions. He already knew the way, as he'd been there before, and reversed out of the parking lot and slowly drove onto the main road. He'd had lunch with a few friends as soon as he'd arrived—they'd picked him up and taken him into town—but now, hours later, he'd left them there with other friends and taken one of the rigs to head to the base. He needed a few moments to get his head together. With any luck this stretch of the journey would give it to him. This was a crappy trip. The only good thing was he had a couple friends he was looking forward to seeing on base too.

He had ten more days in the service, and five of those were compassionate leave. He'd wondered about taking all his leave days here, but, since the compassionate leave was due to his brother's death, it hardly seemed like a good time to tack on vacation time. He was only in Iraq for a short time—just long enough to claim his brother—then to help his father bury Jerry back home.

Parker's military life was almost done, and it seemed like a lifetime to get to that point. He'd never even considered leaving the navy, but now? ... With his accident? ... Followed by his brother's death? ... Parker had hit a wall. He wasn't even sure what the hell he would do when this stage of his life was over. Or even what he was capable of doing.

He'd had a bad accident when the vehicle he was in had rolled. His leg had been pinned, effectively crushing it, and so he was now assigned to a desk job, finding he couldn't stand that.

Parker had a chance of more surgery to help build up his shoulder as well. Something to do with muscles and the scapula. He was really prepared to do that, but he could get it done whether on active leave or not.

What he didn't like was the desk job stuff. If he could get out and be mobile, it wouldn't be so bad, but being on a desk made him feel like he was retired from life. And it had been made clear to him that desk jobs were his future in the military.

Maybe, if he hadn't come from a high-level active military team, he wouldn't feel like he was secondhand goods. Now his life was just a reminder of the one left behind because he couldn't do the job anymore.

As he drove along the road, his brain was consumed with the issues of his future. He thought about Sandy Bressard and her brother. Both of their brothers had died at the same time on the same mission. So Parker and Sandy were both here for a couple days before they took off. He'd heard so much about Sandy but had only met her on the flight here.

They'd spoken briefly and had shared many a glance on their trip, both dreading how painful this process would be, not looking forward to what they had to go through yet. These were hardly ideal circumstances. If she was anything like him, she was blocking out the pain so she could function. Death on the line happened to other families. He'd watched many a friend suffer a personal loss, and he himself had lost several friends, but losing his brother? ... Well, it was just that much harder to deal with.

There would be short ceremonies for the men killed, and then they and their escorting family members were all heading back home. And it sucked. It sucked big-time. Which was why Badger had also said, if Parker wanted something else to think about, to consider this poor dog Samson. He was supposed to go home and retire but had somehow gone missing at the military airport.

It was that *somehow gone missing* part that really bothered Parker because that sounded like a military error or one of those stupid accounting mistakes that had the dog sent someplace other than where he was intended to go. It also bothered Parker because there was a chance somebody had taken the dog deliberately. Well-trained animals were worth a lot of money particularly War Dogs. Parker didn't want to be in the open on enemy lines to face his own war dogs attacking him. He couldn't imagine how confusing that would be for the animals too.

He had another twenty-five minutes to FOB Wild. He was going at a fast clip, but he wasn't late—he was not on a time frame. He should meander, enjoy this last visit. But anything that could make the next couple days go by faster worked for him.

His military-issued jeep wobbled, and, in the next second, he heard a *bang*, felt a hard shake and saw a layer of the tire tread run alongside the road. Swearing softly, he pulled off to the side and hopped out. Sure enough, his back left tire was gone. There was no reason for it. Maybe the tire had shredded, or he had run over something. It happened far enough back that he wasn't bothered about looking for a cause, but he needed to change the tire, and, well, that was never anybody's favorite job.

He had the old tire off and the new one on and the vehicle back down on the ground, putting the finishing tightening turns on the lugs, when he heard another vehicle approaching.

He looked up to see Sandy getting out. She ran over to him, a worried smile on her face. "We left ahead of you," she said, "but we ended up going into town for lunch and lost track of time."

He smiled at the lovely blonde, nodded, and said, "Good. I went into town too, should have stayed longer. I would much rather have been still socializing than changing a tire." But he was joking, and she knew it.

She smiled. "Well, at least you got it fixed. Do you think it's okay now? Is there anything we can do to help?"

"I'm fine," he said, his pride bristling to the surface. Since his accident, he'd become supersensitive to any suggestion that he was less than capable. He stood, brushed off his pant legs, picked up the jack he'd used to change the tire and walked to the end of his vehicle, placing it back in its proper spot. And no way he would let her know his shoulder was less than optimum. It was a hell of a lot better but was a long way from the strength and agility he used to have.

The two women with Sandy were dressed in military fatigues. He nodded at them as he rubbed his hands off on a rag. Sandy explained who he was to her friends, and their expressions changed. They reached out, shook his hand, and said, "Sorry for your loss."

Even now it choked him up. He muttered, "Thank you." Then motioned at the jeep. "Hopefully now it'll get me to the base."

"You go first," said the driver of the other vehicle. "We'll follow to make sure you get there."

Touched, he smiled and said, "Thanks. I'm not too proud to accept that offer. Although I doubt there'll be a problem. It's a new tire."

"Yeah, and we all know that doesn't necessarily mean it's a good tire," Sandy said, a bright smile lighting up her face with the touch of humor.

He laughed, tossing the rag in the back of the jeep. He walked over to the driver's side, slid in and turned on the engine. With a wave, he headed toward the base.

He was surprised Sandy was with these military personnel, but then she had probably met a lot of her brother's friends, and she was also military, though she was a nurse stateside. He wasn't even sure where he got that tidbit of information from. Then, their brothers had been best friends. This was just as painful a trip for her as it was for him, and, if she had friends to make the trip a little easier, all the better for her.

The time flew as he drove. Once he arrived at his destination, he honked his horn and stuck his arm out of his jeep to wave his thanks and turned off into the base. He spotted his buddies' vehicles and parked beside them. He knew which barracks they were in, and he'd been assigned one himself. He grabbed his duffel bag, slung it over his shoulder and headed for his friends.

As he stepped inside, he found the entire barracks empty. Frowning, he picked out his bed, dropped his duffle, left the barracks and headed to the mess tent. He could always count on a cup of coffee, if nothing else.

It was also empty. Frowning, he checked with the guy behind the counter. "Everybody clear out all of a sudden?" he asked. "I hope it wasn't my arrival."

The guy behind the counter grinned at him. "We're on

high alert this morning. Everybody's taken off to check out insurgents, who may or may not have attacked a small group of villagers," he explained.

Parker nodded. "Been there, done that," he said, not surprised. "I presume they went out in waves?"

"They're all over the place," he said. "You know what? If you leave and come back in twenty minutes, this place will have lines out the door with two hundred men and women in here, trying to load up."

"I was just coming for coffee. How many hours until food?" Parker asked, checking his watch, trying to mentally calculate the time difference.

"Two hours," the guy replied helpfully.

Parker nodded, grabbed a large cup of coffee and a muffin, and walked back to his barracks. He could have sat at a table, but it felt odd. He felt odd. He was still one of them and yet, in a way, not one of them. He'd already handed in his notice. He was here to take his brother home, and then Parker was almost done.

Ten days. Five of them were for his brother, and yet how could he explain that to anybody?

He sent a quick text to Badger. **Hey. Arrived. No sign of dog.**

Thanks for the update.

And that was it.

What else was Parker supposed to say? His buddies all knew why Parker was here and that he might start working for Badger when Parker was done here. At least he had told Badger that he was available to help, if Badger needed anything, but they hadn't decided on a specific direction. According to Badger there was always room for another guy at Titanium Corp, but they were based in New Mexico.

Parker was based out of California. Who knew where the hell he'd end up?

He finished his coffee and muffin and tossed the trash. One thing you were taught to do when in the military was to keep your area clean. He headed over to shipping and receiving. As he stepped inside, he smiled at the supply clerk. "I'm here to check on the whereabouts of the dog that went missing."

Her face stiffened. "I can't tell you very much," she said cautiously. "I was told the investigation was closed."

"But the dog hasn't been found, correct?"

"I was told it's closed, pending any further developments," she repeated curtly. "If it is found, it'll be shipped back stateside. I have standing orders to do that, but until I have the dog ..."

"So, did it go missing here, or did it go missing at the air base?"

"At the air base," she replied, looking at him strangely. "It was a really nice dog too."

"Are you thinking maybe somebody took the dog?"

"It wouldn't be the first time things went missing," she muttered.

Considering where she worked, he nodded. "Who took the dog to the base?"

She clicked over to a computer file, brought it up, printed off a page and was about to hand it to him. "I need ID first though."

He looked at her in surprise and pulled out his ID card.

She nodded. "Okay. You're the only one cleared for this information."

He raised an eyebrow.

"Commander Cross called about it," she said with a half

smile. "The K9 war division has been shut down, but you're still checking into a few of his cases, correct?"

He nodded. "At least I can do something worthwhile the last few days before I'm done."

"Are you leaving?" she asked in surprise, her tone almost envious.

"Yes," he said. "I have ten days left. I actually came here to escort my brother's body home, but, while here, I'm looking into Samson's disappearance." He turned with a half wave, grabbed the sheet of paper and walked out.

He read the name on the page. "*Gorman Manga?*" He frowned at that. "What the hell kind of name is that?" he muttered. Then he felt somebody walking behind him.

"There you are," he heard and looked up to see his friend Cam.

They shook hands and slapped each other on the back in a half hug.

Parker grinned and said, "I checked the barracks for you, but you weren't there."

"Nah. I was over with the vehicles. What do you want with Gorman?"

"I'm looking into the dog that disappeared from here."

"That was bizarre," Cam said. "Not that I heard very much about it, just that a dog went missing. Why you?"

"I was asked to." That was one of the things about the military—there were a lot of secrets, and nobody really expected you to tell them the truth about anything because, more often than not, you couldn't.

"Gorman Manga was on that run. And one of his friends but I can't remember his name. Gorman—actually both of them are gone now though. I think they are on leave in Germany," Cam said, frowning.

"His name's really Gorman Manga?"

"Yes," Cam said with a laugh. "He doesn't appreciate it much either. So only tease him if you want to start something."

"Do you know him well enough to ask him about the dog?"

"Sure." Cam pulled out his phone and said, "What do you want to know?"

"How the dog went missing. Apparently it was crated. Did the entire crate get picked up and moved? Is he sure it was latched? Did he sell it or ..."

Cam's eyebrows shot up. "Okay." He walked over a few steps as he made the call. When he ended the call, he turned to Parker. "We caught him still awake. The dog was crated. The team turned away, loading up everything else. The dog would go up front with them. When they finished loading up all the gear and went back to the trolley where the dog was, the front gate to the crate was open, and the crate was empty."

"And he never saw anybody hanging around the place?"

Cam shook his head. "He says not. It was him and two other guys loading and the ground crew."

"I wonder why this dog?"

"Or any dog for that matter," Cam said. "He may have gone in another shipment. Things get busy, and some items get forgotten."

"Maybe. I guess that's one answer. As long as the paperwork was still in order."

"If any of the ground crew was responsible for the lapse, and they catch the dog, I'm sure they would ship him back over again and worry about the paperwork later."

"Pretty slapstick though," Parker said. "If they get

caught, they get shit for the way they handled it."

"It's just a delayed shipment. Hardly a big deal for any-body, except the dog."

"In this case, the dog had an adopted family. I wonder if that has something to do with it."

"I don't know," Cam said. "Anything is possible. When are you leaving again?"

"Late tomorrow," Parker replied. "After the short cere-mony for Jerry and Jeremy tomorrow, we fly back with them in the evening."

Cam's head dropped. "That was a shit deal," he said. "I'm so sorry."

"Me too," Parker said. "If it isn't my brother, it'll be somebody else's for sure."

Cam nodded. "They've both seen way too much in their years over here." Then he grinned. "But you're almost done. I can't believe that. No second thoughts?"

Parker shook his head. "No second thoughts. Jerry's and Jeremy's deaths were the last straw. I'm tired of all the death."

"Gotcha. You still must have plans for the future," Cam said.

"No. I don't," Parker said. "I really don't."

They talked a little bit more while they walked. Parker looked at one of the names on the manifest in front of him for the dog and asked, "What about this other guy. Manfred? Tobey Manfred."

"Tobey's a good guy. He's over in Germany, with Gor-man."

"Okay. And Samson is the only dog that was lost. Cor-rect?"

"I can ask Gorman if anything else went missing, but I

think it was just the dog." He sent a text this time. As they walked, Cam said, "It's almost time for food. We have to get there early. Otherwise you know what happens."

"Sure. Let's go eat. I had coffee and a muffin, but that's been an hour already."

"By the time we get back there and get into line and get through the line, it'll be grub-eating time," Cam said.

They turned around and headed back through the base to the cafeteria. Parker greeted several men he knew as he walked up the line, but only Cam he knew enough to stay with.

By the time they were done eating, Parker looked up, surprised to see Sandy, standing in the middle of the room, searching for a place to sit. He stood and motioned to her. She smiled and walked over. "Hey. Fancy meeting you here. Mind if I join you?"

"No. Not at all," he said. He introduced her to Cam and explained why she was there.

Cam offered his condolences. "I'm sorry for your loss."

She nodded. "It's tough. You don't want to tell anybody why you are here because they don't know what to say."

Cam stood, smiled at them and said, "I'll check in with you later. I've got meetings to go to." And he strode off.

Sandy smiled at Parker. "I'm sorry. I didn't mean to chase him away."

"You didn't," he said. "That's the thing. It feels odd to be here. Like a guest but not quite."

"I was just thinking that as well. I did a couple tours over here, and, now that I'm back for this short time, it feels like I don't really belong. I don't have places to go or people to see. Sure a few but, after an hour or two, it seems like you've said all there is to say. Then it just gets ... awkward.

Everyone tries to avoid broaching the reason we're here, and I don't want to be the first to bring it up. Hell, I don't really want to talk about it at all, but neither do I want my brother to be forgotten."

"Neither do I," Parker said with perfect understanding. "I kind of wish we could go back tonight. I know it's important to be here for the ceremony tomorrow, but …"

She leaned forward. "Me too," she said. "When they said we'd fly in today on the military plane, and then we'd leave a day later, I was kind of like, *Why can't we fly in and fly right out?* I'm good to have it all done in one day. This is tough enough. Why extend the pain? We still have the funerals to go through at home."

"I know," he said. "That'll be a whole other level of hell. On top of that, … I'm leaving the military. I only have ten days left."

She put down her fork. "Don't tell me that your brother was the last straw?"

He stopped chewing in surprise. When he could, he asked, "Why?" And then he knew. "You too?"

"Yes. I've been thinking about it for a long time though," she confessed. "My brother was the one who kept me in all these years. He was such a strong believer, and I am too. The navy has been good for me, but I was thinking it was time to go into the private sector."

"Not too many military people go into the private sector," he said with half a laugh. "Often they join the service and stay for decades, but being in the civilian medical field is an option for you."

"I wasn't so sure I wanted to go back into that, but I know some people who maybe I can work with. A couple private hospitals."

"Right," he said. "I do know somebody connected to a private hospital, but I don't know if they're looking for employees."

"These are my last few official weeks. Then I don't know what …" She pinched the bridge of her nose and sniffled back tears. "I'm sorry."

He grasped her other hand in his and said, "Don't. Don't apologize. We've both lost somebody who mattered to us. This process is difficult enough. We can't try to hide our feelings. We have to acknowledge them and carry on." *Now, if only it were that easy.* But he was damned if he would add to her waterworks by letting his own emotions loose. They'd both end up on a crying jag here and now.

She gave him a half smile. "I don't even want food, but, in the back of my head, I keep hearing a voice that says, *You need your strength. Eat.*"

He agreed, staring at his plate. "I can't see any reason to argue with that common sense. I ate a whole plate of food, and I don't even know what it was."

She took several bites and settled back in her chair, looking slightly more relaxed. She lifted her head from her focus on the plate and asked, "Did you ever learn anything about the dog?"

Grateful for a more neutral and less painful topic, he said, "I spoke to someone. A couple someones. While they were loading the luggage, it seems somebody opened the hatch to the crate and either let the dog out or it escaped on its own. What happened afterward, I don't know. No one does supposedly."

"Right. So, any cameras at the hangar? Anybody have any idea who was hanging around at the time?"

"I need to go to the air base and talk to the ground crew.

The men who took the dog to the air base are on leave in Germany. Although, according to this statement, they both said the dog was there and caged, when they saw it last."

"Any chance they're lying?" Sandy asked in a low tone, looking around to make sure nobody heard them.

Parker felt a start of surprise. He hadn't considered that. Not looking for an ulterior motive from any of the US Navy men here, but it was possible. "That's an interesting thought. I hadn't considered it, but they are both backing up the same story. I guess it depends what the ground crew says."

"Depends on which ground crew. You may have to go there a few times to talk to them all."

Parker glanced at his watch and said, "I thought I'd go tonight. The ceremony is at noon tomorrow, and then we leave."

"Are we leaving tomorrow afternoon or the day after that?" she asked in surprise.

He frowned at her, pulled out his phone and checked it. "Tomorrow, late afternoon, as far as I'm aware."

She pulled out her phone and checked it. "I don't know why I thought it was the day after."

"I'd leave today if I could." He looked at her food left on her plate. "You did well with your meal, after all."

"I feel like puking," she admitted.

"Maybe some fresh air will help. You want to drive with me to the air base again?" He couldn't really explain why, but he didn't want to separate from her right now. Hell, she was literally the only one here who understood him. And what he was going through. They had a bond. And he, for one, wasn't willing to let it go right now. It might be selfish, since he'd originally asked so she wasn't cut loose on her own for the next few hours, but, if he were honest, he'd asked her so he wasn't alone.

"Sure. Why not?" she said with a note of relief in her voice. "It's not like I've got anything here to do. We're both at loose ends, so, if we go together, we might achieve something."

"Maybe one of our last good deeds while we're in the military is to find this dog," he said.

"The dog has already been decommissioned, hasn't it?"

"Yes. If that's what they call it. He was supposed to be adopted by a family in California."

"We're heading back to California, so, if that's the case, maybe we can take him back with us?"

"Maybe," he said with a laugh. "The trouble is, we might get attached and not want to give him up."

"If you find it and rescue it, I'm sure you'll get priority on that one," she said, laughing.

He grinned. "I'm not sure I'm ready for a dog. I don't have a job ten days from now."

"Join the club," she said. They got up from the table, and she reached out her arm and looped it through his. "We're both at new stages of life."

"Right." He nodded. He almost added something then but decided not to. He knew firsthand that, in order to have their new starts, they first had to close the door to the pain in their old lives. And unfortunately, in this instance, it meant closing the door on the life they'd had with their brothers at their sides. They now had to move forward alone, with only their memories to give them comfort.

THEY WALKED ARM in arm back out to his rig, a comfortable peace between them. Sandy looked at their ride and, with a snicker, said, "You think it's safe to trust it?"

"I would think so. After all, it got me here." Parker smirked, loving their ability to joke and to tease each other over the hard underlying reason for both being here. He turned on the engine and headed out of the parking lot.

"Seems so strange," she said. "Being a part of this but on the outside."

"I know. We're here, and yet we don't belong. How long were you in for?"

"Seven years," she replied solemnly. "Seven years. I thought to go ten but after Jeremy ..."

"I hear you. But you have lots of prospects, don't you? There's always a need for medical personnel."

"Yes. I won't have a problem getting a job. At least I don't think so." She glanced at him. "And you?"

"I'm enlisted. For you, it's a different system, right? I'm not sure what I'll do. I have my electrician and plumber licenses, so I could work as a tradesman."

"Yet I'm hearing a *but* in there," Sandy said.

"I was thinking more of building houses and selling them," Parker said with a shrug. "It's what my dad used to do. Heck, it's what my dad still does. Now that my brother's gone, it's just him and me."

"What about your mother?"

"She died when I was seventeen. That sent me into the military."

"Ouch," she said. "I'm lucky. I still have my parents. They're both in the medical field too. Neither were in favor of me going into the military. They're very happy I'm coming home."

"Where's home?"

"Coronado. Or rather, San Diego. I'm sure I'll be leaving my apartment too. It's not on the base, but I'll go wherever the work is."

"Same here," he said. "Amazing how much change has just entered our lives, huh? All from the same sad event."

"Very much so but it's up to us to make the best of it. Where's your father?"

Parker nodded. "The same. San Diego."

"Good," she said. "I won't feel quite so alone then."

He laughed. "No, and you know who to call if you want anybody to build you a house."

She chuckled. "Maybe. Considering the house prices in town …"

"Right," he said. "Seriously crazy. But, if my dad and I can build a few and sell them, maybe that's the way for me to get started." They arrived at the military air base, and he parked near the office end of the hangar and hopped out. "You want to come in with me?"

"Sure," she said. "Anything is better than sitting here alone with my thoughts."

Parker walked in and saw a few guys hanging around the mechanics' area. He grinned. "Almost quitting time?"

They nodded. "Yep."

"Anybody here at the time the dog Samson went missing?"

Two shook their heads, but one nodded.

"I was," he said. "Darnedest thing. A great big shepherd, black all over, sitting in the cage, nice and happy. We finished loading up everything, did the flight checks, turned around to load up the dog, and the cage was there but no dog."

"You didn't see anybody approach?" Parker asked.

The guy, whose tag on his shirt read Ronnie, shook his head. "No. I don't know what happened. Makes no sense. I didn't see the dog running free. I was in the plane for a little bit, moving gear around, but it's not like a bunch of us were here or anything."

"But somebody surely opened the cage, right? It wouldn't accidentally open."

"That's what I figure," he said. "The only way that could happen is if it was one of us. Or a local who saw an opportunity to take him."

The two other men whistled. "That's quite an accusation there, Ronnie," said the one named Drake according to the name tag on his overalls. "It's not like any of us want him. We can't keep him, given where we live."

"All kinds of options though. I'm surprised not more has been done about it," Ronnie said. "That was a nice-looking dog."

"Do you guys ever get approached about dogs for sale or gear for sale on the black market?"

All three nodded. "I think it's a standard thing for anybody in the supply chain and, in our case, because we move items in and out of the country all the time," Drake said. "But it's not just us. The black market is a big machine. I'm sure there are ways to steal things, but it is not worth our jobs or a possible court-martial."

"What would somebody do with a dog like that?" Sandy asked. The men's gaze turned and locked on her.

Ronnie said, "Maybe as a pet, maybe for sale as another military dog, maybe for breeding. Who knows?"

"Anybody leave around that time?" Parker asked, not saying anything about the fact that K9s were always neutered. It made them easier to handle. "I'm just wondering if somebody managed to take the dog. Depending on where you had him caged, it might not have been all that hard to do it. Versus the clasp just popping opening and the dog running away."

Ronnie hopped up, walked over, and said, "We unloaded him here." He pointed to a spot about forty feet from the mechanics' room. "That was where he stayed, until we went back to get him. So it is possible somebody came through here and grabbed him and took him up to the front, but we never did see anybody."

"Do you know of anybody missing whose shift ended around that time?"

Ronnie looked at Parker for a long moment. "And why are you asking?" He walked several steps to the side.

Parker followed. "Because Commander Cross has shut down the War Dogs division and has asked me to take a look into this dog's disappearance. An adopted family stateside is expecting Samson. That dog served a lot of years for the US Navy and deserves a good life."

Ronnie stuck his hands in his pockets. "A kid was hanging around that day," he said quietly. "A local. We would put him to work often, just washing up stuff for a few bucks. I haven't seen him since."

"Do you have a name?"

"Anatol," he said. "He's from the village on the other side of that hill."

Parker nodded. "Was he a good kid?"

"Honestly, I'd say he was. I'm hoping he didn't take the dog for meat, but it's possible. He was hungry enough."

Parker winced. "I sure hope not. That's a very expensive canine roast."

"I think he knew Samson was worth more money, but

Anatol was also pretty googly-eyed over any of the animals that came through here. A real animal lover. So I don't think that was his end in mind."

"Let me see if I can find the dog before I leave for home."

"And when is that?"

"I'm flying out tomorrow, as it stands now. If possible, I'd like to take the dog back with me. We'll head out there now. See if we can find Anatol or Samson."

"Tell him Ronnie sent you."

"Did you know what happened at the time?"

Ronnie's back went up.

Parker shook his head. "I don't care. I'm not part of it. I'm out of the military in a few days. My whole job is to take my brother's body home and hopefully a live dog."

Ronnie relaxed a bit and said, "I saw the kid, and then the dog disappeared around the same time. Haven't seen either since. Draw your own conclusion." And he walked away.

CHAPTER 2

A S SOON AS Parker and Sandy returned to their vehicle and headed out," Sandy asked, "What was that about?"

"He may have an idea where the dog is," Parker said and explained the little he'd learned.

"And he didn't tell anyone?" she asked in outrage.

"I'm not sure what that is about either," he said. "Ronnie didn't seem to think the kid would hurt the dog, but that's not the same issue."

"No," she said. "He doesn't know for sure that the dog is okay, nor does he know for sure that the kid took the dog."

"I know. Maybe the kid loved the dog, but that doesn't mean that any adults around here will let him keep it."

Sandy sagged back in her seat. "Can we go to the village and see? It's still early."

"Sure," Parker replied. "I was planning to and hoped you'd be okay with it."

"We might as well have something to do," she said, "rather than sitting around, waiting for the myriad of emotions to hit us unexpectedly."

"Yeah, ain't that the truth." He changed directions and headed off toward the village. "I hope it's not too far away."

"If the kid's coming here cross-country, his home can't be more than a few miles away. Likely he grabbed the dog, then led him back the same way. Unless he's driving, and I don't know about that, given he's a kid, but it's possible, since no one said he was alone."

It was a five-minute drive to the village. Parker slowed down as they approached. Just one main street and a couple side streets. He said in a low voice, "Look for the dog."

It wasn't as if Sandy needed to be told twice; she had been searching for any animals since they'd left the hangar. She pointed out several dogs, but they were nothing like the big shepherd Samson. They got to the other end of the street and saw a young man walking. Parker pulled off to the side and hopped out to speak with him.

Sandy watched the animated discussion, and the man pointed up the road. Parker returned and started up the engine. Sandy asked, "Does he know where the dog is?"

"He saw the dog with the kid, but then he said a group of men came."

"Uh-oh," she uttered.

He nodded. "Like I said, if the dog has any value, the kid can't keep it. Out here, only the strong win that battle."

"That's too bad," she said. "I forget sometimes just how Americanized we are."

"It's a different world here. Poverty is everywhere." He drove farther up the road and came to what looked like another settlement. He parked, got out and walked over to a door. An older woman came to meet him. She didn't speak English from the look of the conversation. Sandy stared out the front window, trying to understand what was being discussed, concentrating hard, until somebody rapped on the window beside her, and she let out a shriek. She turned and rolled down the window. "Hi," she said, drumming up a smile. "We're looking for a large shepherd."

The frown deepened on the middle-aged man, but his

eyes darted to the side.

Her gaze followed his to a young boy. She pushed her door open, sending the man back slightly. She called to the little boy, "Are you the one who took the shepherd?"

The man beside her spoke urgently. "He knows he did wrong," he said, holding out his hand for the boy to come closer. "He wanted to take the dog back, but it was too late. The cage wasn't latched, and, when he called out to the dog, the dog pushed the gate open, then hopped down and raced toward him. He took that as the dog wanted to come away with him."

She glared at the little boy, leaning against his father. "Where is the dog now?"

The boy looked to the father. "A group of men came and took the dog," he whispered.

"What did they want the dog for?"

The boy shrugged.

But she could see the worry in his eyes. He had to be twelve, maybe a little younger. The typical age of those who hung around the base, hoping for a chance to deliver water or to get a few coins for a simple job. "Did you recognize these men?"

The boy nodded his head.

Sandy crossed her arms over her chest and looked at Parker, who seemed to realize something was going on and joined them. When he arrived, she explained.

Parker pushed his fingers through his hair. "Where can we find these men?"

"That's not a good idea," the boy's father exclaimed. "The men are dangerous."

"That's why you gave them the dog?" she asked. "It was a stolen dog. You know that, right? Stolen from the base," she added for clarity.

The father winced, looked at the little boy, watching the boy's shoulders as they sagged.

"Just because you want a dog doesn't mean you can have the dog," she said gently. "Thousands of dollars went into his training. He was going home, where he should have started a good life of retirement. Instead he's been kidnapped by these men, who could have done anything from kill him to use him to terrorize other people."

Parker turned to the father. "Where can I find these men?"

The father pointed up the road. Parker wanted to know how far. The man shrugged. The discussion went back and forth a little bit more; then, finally, the little boy said something about rebels.

Parker looked down at him. "You think they're up at a rebel hideout?"

The boy nodded his head.

"Have you seen the dog since?"

The little boy shook his head.

Sandy felt sad for the little boy who badly wanted a dog, but, at the same time, she felt worse for the dog. Samson was very valuable, but no way would the military pay a ransom to get him back, especially not since he was being decommissioned. She turned to face Parker. "Do you want to drive ahead and take a look, then return to the base for backup?"

She watched as he fisted his hands on his hips, glaring at the world around him. She didn't like the answers any more than he did. To go into a rebel holdout alone was suicide. But it wasn't as if they would get any backing either. "I suggest we take a look," she said. "Obviously we won't get too close. We don't have any weapons."

He nodded. "Exactly." He glanced at the boy. "Do you know where they live?"

The little boy nodded. He glanced at his father.

"Any idea how many men?" There was a discussion about the men, the weapons, how far away they were and how much difficulty they made for the villagers' lives. Anything this group of people had, the rebels came through and took.

No love was lost between the groups. Parker couldn't blame them. These villagers worked hard for anything they had, and to have a group like that come through and just take what they wanted would never sit well. Thanking them, he got back into the vehicle, and Sandy hopped into the passenger side.

As they drove up the road, she said, "The little boy looks devastated."

"Of course he does. Not only did he take a chance and do something that was wrong and grab a US Navy dog but now he lost it too. And he's probably put his whole family in jeopardy."

"It's a terrible thing," she said. "I wonder why they wouldn't let him have one."

"I don't know," Parker said. "They might rethink that issue now. Maybe they'll realize he needs to be punished, and he definitely won't get one because he tried to steal one. But stealing from the military base is bad news. He's probably afraid he can't go back to the base. That's how a lot of them make money."

"I remember," Sandy said. "Always a dozen local kids were around, willing to go and get us water or food or whatever was asked."

Parker smiled and nodded. "There used to be a regular

group. And I'm sure we were the reason those families survived."

"Right?" she said, leaning back, holding up her hand to shade her eyes from the bright sun as it started to set. "It's amazing, when you look back on the months you spent here, how it became so normal. And then you return stateside, and you don't see the urchin street kids anymore. You don't see people making a living off delivering water." She shook her head. "It's like apples to oranges, and yet, at the same time, it really makes you realize just how privileged we are."

"I'm not missing this," Parker said. "I spent too many months here. And it feels like a lifetime ago, and I feel like a stranger, even now."

"Well, we've just arrived," she said. "So, as far as being a stranger, ... that's due to our unique circumstances."

"Exactly, and it would normally take a couple days to get adjusted, and then, all of a sudden, it would seem like I had never left. I didn't really like that. It should feel vastly different and stay that way. Instead it all blurs into an existence that's no longer different. There's such an odd sensation to know that you could fall back into any given norm so quickly."

They kept driving until Parker pulled off the roadside near a large tree. "Would you mind if I got out and walked a little bit? I want to take a closer look."

She studied this face. "I'm going with you. Don't even think about telling me to stay behind. But why did you pull off here?"

"Because I saw a light up there," he said. "Chances are they are looking at us, and I just wanted to pull off to the side as if we were sitting here intentionally. And I'm not ordering you, but I need you to stay behind."

Damn. She glared at him. "Not fair. And how the hell will you get out without them noticing? You shouldn't be up there alone."

He smiled. They were driving a navy jeep without a rear window and open sides. Still, he slid over the back of his seat into the rear seat, then snuck out the back door on her side. Next thing she knew, he was among the trees and dashing up the hillside.

"I guess I'm not going after all," she said out loud, watching him disappear from sight. She wasn't scared. Never really had been out here, yet that awareness of rebels around was always with her. War was a constant fear factor which you became dulled to after a while. She stared at the bushes where she'd last seen Parker. How long would he be?

PARKER USED THE ground cover to his advantage, crawling up the hill far away from where he'd seen the light. As he crested the top, he could see a little bit of a rise, and nestled on the other side were several huts and small buildings. A compound with dogs was around the back. He was too far away to see if the shepherd was there, but it would make sense that, if these guys had the shepherd, it would be with the other dogs.

Time was tight. He didn't want to leave Sandy too long. He'd rather not leave her alone at all. It would be inexcusable to have something happen to her from this decision. But the opportunity was here. And if there was one thing he'd learned from his navy days, it was to make the most of those.

Making a quick decision, he slid down the hill along the back behind the dog compound. As he approached the fence, he saw a big black male shepherd. He gave a slight whistle that he knew the dog should have heard many times in the military. The dog jumped to its feet and came racing to the back fence. Parker gave a second whistle on a different octave, wondering if the dog was capable of jumping to that level. The dog, from a standstill, soared over the fence and ran toward him. Parker had no lead for him, but, carefully maneuvering back the same way he came, Parker slid down the hill on the other side, keeping the dog at his side.

Once they got to the trees, he stopped and hugged the dog. Samson still had a collar on him with his name. Parker crept to the jeep, holding the dog by the collar.

Sandy stared at him. "That easy?"

"It's never that easy," he said. Just then shots were fired over his head. He swore and got the dog into the back seat of the jeep.

Before he could head to the driver's side, Sandy slid over and already had the jeep running. "Get in, get in."

He jumped into the passenger side. At his feet, he found a piece of rope for a lead for the dog.

Sandy drove like a crazy person, leaving a huge plume of dust behind them. As they hit the small village, everybody was already undercover and hiding, but Parker knew people were coming after them.

"We have to be prepared for them to gain on us," he cried out as he watched behind them.

Sandy gave him a startled look and yelled, "I'm going as fast as we can."

He nodded. "After the village we have to find a place to hide. We don't want to hide close to the village, in case the rebels attack the villagers."

"No, that's not happening," she said. "If we can get to

the base or to the airport, that would be the best."

He nodded. "They were at least prepared for us. I don't have any weapons. Do you?"

"No," she said. "I wasn't issued one. I'm just here as a visitor. Remember?"

"I know. Me too," he said. "Doesn't matter what we used to do. It's what we currently do that matters." He looked behind them to see a vehicle coming faster than they could drive. "Do you want me to take over?" he yelled.

She shook her head and noticed the vehicle behind them. "I can drive faster."

"Go cross-country. We should be able to lose them on the other side of the village."

She didn't hesitate.

He really admired that. She took directions and drove fast. She twisted the wheel hard and blazed cross-country. The road was a lot rougher, but, as long as she could avoid any big rocks, they should gain some speed. The road returned not too far ahead, and he pointed it out to her. She nodded and angled toward it, and, with a heavy jump, the vehicle ripped up onto the road again, landed roughly and peeled away. He looked over to see Samson, his tongue lolling, facing the wind, as if enjoying the ride.

"Is the dog okay?" she asked.

"He's better than okay," Parker said with a big grin. "I think he's enjoying this."

"Of course. This is his deal, isn't it?" She laughed. "But you realize, if it isn't the right dog, we're the ones in the wrong here."

"It's the right dog," he said. "I checked his tag."

"Well, thank God for that." Just then the same black vehicle ripped up in the road not too far behind them.

Parker swore. "They took the same shortcut."

She glanced in the rearview mirror, and he could see the fear in her eyes.

"Just drive, drive, drive," he said.

The trouble was, they were being fired upon now. It wouldn't be long before the rebels were close enough to hit their target. Parker looked for options. They had to find some way out of this. "Maybe the airport," he said.

"Sure. Do you have a way to get there cross-country? At least that way maybe they'll hit a rock or get caught up in something versus us," she said. "On the road, it's all about speed."

"That's very true," he said. He studied the ground around them and pointed up ahead. "At that second corner, go over. It'll be terrifying because of the sharp rise initially, but it smooths out really fast."

"And you know this how?"

"Because I used to do a lot of driving here. I know this area fairly well. We can head to the airport completely cross-country from there, catch it on the far side of one of the runways and drive all the way in."

"I like the sound of that," she said with a laugh.

Another shot was fired at them and pinged the vehicle on the side. She swore.

"Steady. We're coming up to the spot ..."

She kept driving straight ahead until Parker cried, "Now."

She sent the vehicle straight off the edge of the corner.

CHAPTER 3

SANDY'S HEART RACED, and she would swear to God that she'd never driven like this in her life. Just taking that vehicle over the edge was enough to give her a heart attack. But she hung on, her foot hard on the gas as the vehicle raced magically forward.

Parker was laughing at her side. "Good girl," he said, his voice full of admiration.

She shook her head. "I was absolutely terrified."

"Terrified but you did it anyway," he said. "And that's what this is all about. Courage is being brave when you're under fire. You've definitely got what it takes. Watch out for that big boulder coming up."

But she had this now. She twisted around the boulder and kept going, picking out the path in front of them.

"Where did you learn to drive?"

She laughed. "My brothers," she said. "They taught me. They were all about 4x4-ing. I can't say we ever raced like this, but cross-country driving is second nature. Just not under this kind of pressure. Or speed. Or gunfire."

"The faster, the better," Parker said. "We can make up a lot of time this way."

Another shot pinged, making her duck instinctively. But then nothing else came, and she eased the tension in her shoulders while she raced ahead as fast as the terrain allowed.

If it wasn't for the danger, she'd be thoroughly enjoying herself.

Parker stretched his arm out and pointed. "Turn up here. Your ten o'clock."

She turned the steering wheel and headed in that direction.

He laughed. "You're good at this."

"Nope. I'm *great* at this," she said smugly. "I used to navigate for my brothers whenever we went out driving. I've done this plenty. We loved the dunes the best. Who knew my misspent childhood would come in so handy?"

"Now that would be fun," he said, chuckling. "Coming up, I want you to do a two-o'clock turn. Right ... now."

She turned again. "Now we're going back the same way we were," she said. "Did you consider that?"

"I know," he said. "But that's all right because this is where we need to be."

Almost instantly she took the vehicle up a small rise and jumped over the top and blasted onto smooth ground. She cried out in surprise.

"Hit the gas, and go fast," he said.

"Ha, I'm going as fast as I can." She already had her foot flat on the floor, racing toward the small buildings ahead. "I don't know how you saw this in this light," she said. "I can barely see."

"I know, and it'll just get worse. I'm glad we did this when we could. In a way, it was a perfect storm that worked in our favor."

"How's the dog?"

"Samson is fine," Parker replied. "I swear he's enjoying this."

She checked the dog, and, sure enough, he was sitting up

in the back seat, looking around. "Doesn't seem like anything fazes him."

"Think about his training. Think about what he's seen. Think about what he's been through …"

"Good point," she said. "Are they still behind us?"

He checked the rearview mirror. "Doesn't look like it. It's clear."

As they came up to the small air base, Sandy said, "Nobody'll be here, will they?"

"Not likely at this time. Let's drive up to the hangar, where we were last. We need a place for Samson to stay for the night. This might be our best bet."

"But that means we have to stay with him too," she said. "No way we can trust anybody else with the dog. Not at this stage. I'm still not sure Ronnie didn't help the kid take the dog by leaving his cage unlatched."

"You got that, huh? I was wondering myself," he said.

Sandy slowed down and pulled up against the hangar door. Parker hopped out and disappeared from sight. She drove a little past, looking for any place to pull out of sight because the last thing she wanted was somebody to follow her here. She parked around the corner and turned to pet Samson. The big shepherd whined, then licked her hand and nudged her to give him a better scratching. She scrubbed him hard, chuckling. "Aren't you a beautiful boy," she whispered.

He barked at her, almost like a yes.

Parker came back. "One of the side doors is open," he said. "Let's take him in there." He wrapped his hand around the rope and led Samson out of the back of the jeep. They went around to the side door.

Sandy checked the surrounding area, looking for any

plume of dust, indicating if vehicles were coming their way, but she saw nothing. She turned to Parker. "You know they're out there."

He nodded. "Oh, yeah. They definitely are."

PARKER OPENED THE hangar door quietly and slipped inside, holding Samson at his side, Sandy with him. He whispered against her ear, "I don't want to turn on the lights, in case we're seen."

She nodded. "Any way we can open the bay door to bring in the jeep?"

He pondered that for a moment and then nodded. "I think we have to take that risk. The rebels are likely to come here anyway, but, if they find the vehicle outside, they'll know for sure and likely disable it."

He walked over to one of the big bays and studied it. "What I need is a manual crank," he said. "So we don't have to fire up the electronics, which could be noisy."

He studied the panel on the side, hit a few buttons, switching off the auto functions. He grabbed one of the handles and pulled. It took a little more effort than he expected, but it did lift. Halfway up, he studied the height and realized the jeep should just about make it through. He fired it up, and, without turning on its lights, then shutting off the jeep's running lights, he backed it up and parked it inside the hangar.

He shut off the engine and let out a breath. He jumped out and pulled the door closed as quietly as he could. He couldn't see anything out there from where he stood. He heard Sandy's strangled call.

"Parker?"

"I'm here," he said. "What's up?" He could hear a whine coming from Samson.

"What's the matter?" he repeated, walking toward the sound. He pulled out his phone and turned on the flashlight. He shone it on her face, seeing a strange look.

She said, "Look down."

He shone the flashlight around to see a man crumpled facedown on the floor.

"Shit," he said, dropping to the man's side. He checked for a pulse but found nothing. A large pool of blood was under his chest and abdomen area. Shining the flashlight on his face to confirm, he had already recognized who it was. "It's Ronnie."

She nodded and whispered back. "Yeah. I recognized him."

He looked at her, and she shrugged. "When you opened up the garage door to come in, I saw just enough. Did you check how he died?"

He shone the flashlight over the body again.

"Exit wound," she said and pointed to the center of his back.

Twisting the flashlight for a better angle, he nodded. "Single bullet hole."

"But, if that was the case, that would turn the suspects into the two people that were here when we talked to him earlier."

"That's an assumption we can't afford to make," he cautioned. "He could also have stayed behind and spoken to somebody or had a private meeting here."

"Do you think it's related to Samson?"

"The dog could be part of it, but I suspect this is just the tip of the iceberg." Sandy stared at him, and he nodded. "Too much potential here for selling and stealing contraband."

"You mean, the ground crew removing items that are supposed to be shipped in or out?" she asked. "All of that paperwork is checked and cross-checked many times."

"Sure, but by whom?"

She sagged to the ground beside Ronnie, as if not wanting to leave the dead man alone. "I suppose if one had a system in place," she said slowly, "it'd be all too possible."

"Not only possible but likely," he said, searching her face in the dim light. She was holding firm. Shaken but standing her ground. All the more reason to admire her. He reached out a hand. She reached back. "Unfortunately it happens all the time. Not necessarily from the ground crew or from anybody flying in or out, but, within the military base itself. Humans make honest mistakes. Plus the paperwork is daunting. So consider how many moving parts are necessary to keep track of. Stealing military supplies to resell is big business. It's very easy for somebody to set up a system like this."

"So now what do we do?" she asked, standing up, holding on to his hand.

"That's a good question. Because we have to contact the right person." Then he added, "And *only* the right person."

He could feel her twist as she turned her head to look at him again. He shuffled over a step and tugged her closer, almost in his arms, and he added, "We have to make sure, if this goes as far as the rebel camp, which it probably does, that we don't contact the wrong person somehow who is already involved."

"Meaning, if they've already killed one person, what's

several more? Do you think it's that lucrative to risk the penalties?" She turned slightly to look at the darkened hangar, as if someone were listening in.

"I think it's beyond lucrative," he said quietly. "Smuggling always is. And when it's Uncle Sam's goods, potentially moving to rebels in this country or another, I think those types of items are worth their weight in gold."

"Oh, good Lord. What did we get into?"

"It's me that's into it," he said. "I promise I'll get you back to the base. You can leave tomorrow. That's the plan."

"We've already been seen together," she said in a reasonable tone, as if trying to explain something he wasn't already aware of.

The trouble was, he was very much aware of how much danger he'd put her in. He tugged her closer. She came willingly, snuggling in for warmth. "I should never have asked you to come," he said. "I was just thinking about a nice country drive, looking for a dog and getting off the base for a bit. Something to take our minds off the real reason we're here."

"We were both thinking that," she said. "The base holds tough memories for us, and both our brothers are lying back on the base, waiting to be flown home. I wanted to get away just as much as you."

"Right," he said. "We found Samson too." He reached out and scratched Samson on the back of the head. Samson lay down beside him and dropped his head on Parker's foot.

"The question is, what do we do now?" she asked.

"I'm also wondering that. Not just what to do now but I'm wondering whether or not the dog saw something. I know that sounds foolish, but these dogs are trained. In many different areas. Maybe he alerted someone who shouldn't have been alerted, or maybe he smelled something that shouldn't have been smelled. Or maybe Ronnie befriended the kid and thought he should have a dog of his own and let Samson loose."

"Let the dog loose?" she reiterated slowly. "Right. No way that kid would have been allowed out of here on the runway with Samson, would he?"

Parker looked at her. "Not likely, but that doesn't mean impossible," he said.

"The dog was used to being flown around the country," she said with a frown. "Which means, where the dog was located at the time of his disappearance was actually part of this. Because, if he was already on board the plane, the local boy couldn't get a hold of Samson."

"Even if Samson was in the hangar here," he said, "I highly doubt the boy could open the cage, unless somebody had left it open for him. Like Ronnie. Or potentially someone saw the kid here and thought he'd make a great scapegoat."

"And, if the boy didn't take Samson, the dog could have run off anyway."

"Potentially, yes," he said. "But you also have to consider that most likely men were here who could have controlled the dog with commands."

"Except that he was now being sent home for retirement. He didn't have a handler with him, besides the Gorman guy."

"Gorman and his buddy. They have both said the dog was close to the plane but how close? I don't know." He pulled out his phone. "I want to ask Cam a few more questions about that, but I don't want to alert anyone here. So I can't contact my buddy."

"We have to do something," Sandy said, tilting her head back to look up at him. In the darkness he could barely make out her features; only the whites of her eyes showed. And the fear darkening them.

"Yes, but we have to bring in somebody from the outside. And that's tricky."

"Okay, so not Commander Cross, without jumping to a lot of unfounded and unsubstantiated conclusions. What about the guy who asked you to come look for the dog?" she asked. "He should have connections."

"That might not be the worst idea," he said. He stepped aside slightly, keeping an arm around her shoulders and hit Badger's name on his contact list. He listened as the phoned dialed the number. When Badger answered, Parker said, "I've got a problem."

"Let me have it," Badger said. "Problems are the name of our game."

"I hope so because this one is ugly," Parker replied and explained the issue.

CHAPTER 4

SANDY LISTENED TO the conversation as she crouched and studied the dead man in front of her. She reached up to grab Parker's hand as it slid off her shoulder. She didn't want to lose that physical connection. They were close together, but it wasn't the same as being tucked up against him. The man on the ground wasn't the real problem. No, she'd seen more than her fair share of death; it was part of her career, but it was also part of her military career.

She'd been months on the front lines, and she'd helped save a lot of men, but a lot of men came to her too far gone to save. None of it was easy. But finding this man killed in cold blood on a US Navy base bothered her more than anything. And the nuances that were yet to be sorted out here were something else again. She'd come for her brother and had somehow gotten embroiled in something much uglier. And this poor man, someone she'd spoken with just hours earlier, was gone. Such a waste.

He'd been a young, vibrant man just a few hours ago. And to see him cut down like this, and for what? Revenge to keep quiet because he'd opened his mouth? Because he'd let Parker know about the local boy? Because he'd helped let the dog escape? None of them were good enough reasons for her. When she heard silence behind her, she turned to look at Parker. "So?"

"He'll contact Commander Cross. And then he'll get back to me."

Not even five minutes later, both of them sitting in the dark, waiting, his phone buzzed. "Badger. What'd you find out?"

Sandy leaned in so she could hear the call. "Commander Cross has contacted the base commander. Colonel Barek says a special military police force is coming your way. It'll be four men. He's vetted them all, but Commander Cross said, as we well know, deceit happens. Even at the highest level. So he wants you to keep an eye on the MPs, get their names and monitor their actions closely."

"Once they get here, we're cut out. You know that, right?" Parker said.

"Yes," Badger said. "So, you have about twenty minutes. I suggest you take a look around for clues."

"We've deliberately been hiding because of the rebels chasing us."

"Any rebels coming now will meet up with the military police. You got twenty minutes."

"Got it," Parker replied and ended the call. He shot to his feet and said, "We're supposed to look for anything out of the ordinary. And we need to take pictures. I'll let you do that."

"Of what?"

He turned to look at her. "Everything," he replied quietly.

She nodded. He hit the lights, and she started at the entrance, taking photos of everything inside the hangar, including full exterior pictures of the vehicles and the equipment and the internal layout of the building. She finished doing a panoramic view of floor to ceiling and then wall to wall. That took longer, and she could feel the time constraints pulling at her. She wanted more photos, but, just as she finished taking more shots of the body, she heard the sound of vehicles arriving. "Parker?"

"I hear them," he said. "Stay calm."

"Easy for you to say." She turned back to the body, took several more pics of him and his position, even though she knew it was probably useless, and then sat back down beside Parker.

Just then came a voice outside. "Military police. Stand down. We're coming through."

Parker called back. "The door is open. Come on in. We've been waiting for you." The door slammed open, but nobody entered. Parker walked over so they could see him, his hands in the air. Four men filed in, holstering two weapons but still within an easy reach. They took one look at the empty building and walked over to where Sandy sat. She stood and was asked for her identification.

Parker was ahead of them. He gave their names, ranks and reason for being there.

"This is a long way from where your brothers lie," said the first man, Bobby Telford according to his ID. "What are you doing here?"

"You can confirm with Commander Cross," Parker replied. "A K9 shepherd went missing several months ago during the transfer to the military plane taking him home. Commander Cross, knowing I would be here to collect my brother and also knowing I am part of the Titanium Corp, asked if I could spend a day or two looking for the whereabouts of the dog. As you can see, that is the dog right there."

Samson even now sat at attention beside the dead man.

Sandy reached down and scratched him. He snuggled a

little closer to her leg, as if unsure of the current situation. Or maybe he was getting the same vibes as her. Because she definitely felt uncertain. The two men who entered last walked around and did a complete search of the hangar.

Parker, as succinctly as he could, gave an explanation of what they were doing here at that moment.

When he was done, she commented, "Honestly, we were just getting off the base and away from the heavy memories."

The men nodded. "I'm sorry for your loss," Telford said. "War has a habit of causing a lot of pain."

Sandy motioned to Ronnie in front of them. "We spoke to him not two hours ago."

Telford asked her to go over the conversation. She did, to the best of her ability, checking with Parker to see if he had anything to add.

Parker shook his head. "He's the one who told us about the local boy. We headed out toward the village, found the boy and his father, and learned the rebels had the dog. I went in, grabbed the dog, came back. Simple."

"Well. Not so simple," Telford replied with a disgusted tone. "Not if you brought in a group of rebels on our heads."

"I drove straight here on his directions," Sandy said, motioning at Parker. "And thank God for that. Because the rebels were shooting at us all the way down the road, as you can see by the bullet holes in the jeep. But, once we went cross-country and came upon the airstrip, I think they stopped following us. They were likely afraid they'd be up against more than they were ready to handle. If we hadn't come tonight, Ronnie would have been here all night, not found until the morning."

The MPs nodded. Two stood off to the side, making phone calls, and Sandy remained motionless, not happy about all the weapons they carried. But then she'd spent enough time around active duty personnel that she shouldn't be bothered. But it was the first time she herself was involved in an investigation.

"Did you know Ronnie prior to coming here this evening?" Telford asked.

"No," she said. "Not that I recall. I've done a lot of tours in Iraq. His face is not familiar, nor is his name."

"Good enough." The lead MP looked at both of them and said, "Somebody will give you a ride back to the base."

She frowned, but he gave no indication he was willing to argue. She slid her hand under Samson's rope, keeping him by her side. The two closest MPs looked at the dog, then looked over at Parker.

Parker said, "The dog is going stateside with us tomorrow."

Telford nodded slowly. "He needs to be cleared for that."

"I'm sure Commander Cross is on it," Parker said.

WITH BADGER'S WORDS in mind, Parker quietly, trying not to bring any attention to what he was doing, took photos of each of the four MPs. Then he typed in their names and sent them off to Badger.

He didn't know if that would do any good. One of the men noticed what he did. "Do we need to confiscate your phone?" he asked, his voice hard.

Parker looked at him. "You're more than welcome to. I just sent your names to Badger from Titanium Corp, who is in direct contact with Commander Cross. Obviously we have some suspicions of an inside job here, and we're making sure you four are on the up-and-up."

They were greeted with stony silence across the room.

"Of course Commander Cross is already in contact with the base commander, who sent you four MPs here. So you can look at me as a suspect if you want, but I'm looking right back at you as suspects as well." He knew he shouldn't have said that because all four men stiffened and glared at him. He shrugged and said, "Look at it from my point of view."

"And from ours," the first man said, his voice calm but authoritative.

Parker nodded. "Exactly. We'll take the dog back to the base. There's no crate for him here. I'll try and get one from the K9 supplies, and we'll get him shipped out with us tomorrow."

"As long as we have your contact information. And you don't leave the base until we complete our investigation."

"As long as your investigation is completed by the time we leave with our brothers," Sandy said, walking toward Parker, Samson at her side, "then we agree. It's not as if you'll have trouble finding us stateside."

The men looked at each other and then nodded. "Johnson here will take you back to the base," Telford said.

Parker agreed.

Johnson separated from the group, and they all headed outside to the vehicle the MPs had arrived in.

"What about our vehicle?"

"Leave it. One of the men will bring it back."

Without an option, Parker sat in front, and Sandy sat in the back with Samson. The dog showed no sign of unrest, but his gaze was wary of the new scenario. His life had flipped in the last few months.

They drove the short distance back to the base. Nobody said a word until the vehicle pulled into the parking lot. Parker hopped out; Sandy and Samson followed. They stopped, looked down at the dog, and Parker said, "I'm not sure I can take him into the regular barracks."

Johnson nodded. "Arrangements have been made. Go see Colonel Barek first. I'll take you there." He shut off the engine, hopped out and led the way.

As they walked into the colonel's office, Parker and Sandy straightened, saluted and waited to be addressed.

The colonel looked up at Parker and frowned. "I've spoken to Commander Cross and to Badger. You two got yourself in a hell of a pickle."

Parker raised an eyebrow and gave a short nod.

"You do, however, appear to have found the missing K9 dog, Samson. Is that correct?" He stared at the dog between the two of them. "Good. That's one thing we needed to clear up. But you've also brought the rebels back to the base, I understand?"

Sandy shook her head. "No, sir. That is not correct. They stopped firing at us miles out, then stopped following us a couple miles before the air base. I think they knew we were returning to the base."

"The question is, was the dog worth them coming after you again?"

"Potentially," she said. "But, since the dog had come from the base, I'm sure they understood the ramifications of attacking us over a dog they had no right to."

"Exactly," he said. "I understand from Johnson you potentially have a dispute with us?"

"Not necessarily," Parker said. "But Ronnie's death appears to be more of an inside job, and I didn't want to hand over this information to somebody who might be part of it."

The colonel tossed down the pencil he had in his hand and crossed his arms as he leaned back on the desk. "Tell me why you think that?" he invited.

Parker hesitated, and then, with a look at Sandy, he explained the little he knew.

"You think we have a smuggling issue going on here?"

Parker nodded.

"Well, I'm glad you're going home tomorrow," the colonel said. "I wish it was for better reasons than what you were here for. But you are correct. We do have a problem, and this could be part of a much bigger issue. Unfortunately it has now cost the life of that young man, and I want to make sure that no more lives are lost in this investigation."

Parker was surprised at the colonel's admission. But then it wasn't as if it was something to hide now.

"Glad to leave, sir. Obviously this is a delicate issue."

"It is, indeed." The colonel looked at them each and with a stern look, said, "I presume I can count on your silence?"

Parker nodded once. Sandy nodded as well.

The colonel continued, "I don't want you talking to anybody, and not because I don't trust you but because I know what a base is like for gossip. To that end, I've placed the three of you in the same lodgings. Is that an issue?"

Parker could feel Sandy's startled reaction. He looked at her and then said, "I'm fine with it, sir."

She nodded. "That's fine, sir. Thank you."

"Samson's to stay with you. We'll get him a crate. He is to be crated at all times, except when he needs to relieve himself. Do you understand?"

Parker didn't think it was very fair but agreed. "Is there a reason for that, sir?"

"Yes. We lost the damn dog once, and he's back to being my responsibility until he's off this base. So, until that point, he stays in his crate." He made a motion, letting them know they were dismissed.

Parker turned and led the way out of the office. With Samson still attached to the rope in his hand, Parker stood outside and took several deep breaths.

Sandy muttered right beside him, "What is it about standing in front of the big boss that makes everything else go hazy?"

Parker chuckled. "Well, we shouldn't be in trouble over this, although Samson won't enjoy the next twenty-odd hours."

"Right? That's a long time for a dog in a crate."

"We have to make sure we get a big one so he can stand up, move around, lie down comfortably. We'll take him out for a lot of breaks."

She chuckled. "Of course. I can help with the breaks."

"Yes," he said. "Now we find out where we're supposed to stay."

"Isn't it odd that they want us together?"

"Everything about this trip has been odd," he said in a low tone. He motioned at the MP coming toward them. "Looks like Johnson is on our case."

Johnson stopped in front of them and said, "Follow me, please." He led the way to a small portable barracks. It was empty except for themselves. On one side of the first bed was a large crate. Johnson said, "This will be your room. Please don't leave it until you're called for breakfast in the morning."

"And if we do?" Sandy asked in surprise. "I have friends

on base I'd hoped to spend some time with. What about walking the dog? He has needs too."

"All visits have been curtailed. You're expected to stay in these lodgings. We will post security if need be. As for the dog, you can walk him outside at the entrance in full sight of the sentries only." With that, he turned and walked away.

Inside the barracks, Parker and Sandy stared at each other. "Are we prisoners?" she asked.

"I think they're just making sure we don't get into any more trouble," Parker replied. "And it definitely reinforces how I feel about staying in the military."

"Right, and that's likely to be as much of the reason why they're doing this too," she said with a nod of her head. "I didn't really consider that."

"Right. From their point of view, we're already outsiders."

"Yeah. So which bunk do you want?"

He chuckled and said, "There are lots of spares. Pick one."

She picked the one across from where the crate was and threw herself down. "What about dog food?"

"We should have asked Johnson to bring some," Parker said, rubbing Samson's ears. "I think I'll step outside and see what kind of response we get."

She laughed. "Better you than me. But crate up Samson before somebody comes in and finds out you're not following orders."

He groaned. "Samson probably needs to lift a leg. We also don't know when he was last fed." And, with Samson once again at his side, Parker stepped out of the barracks.

CHAPTER 5

S ANDY WAITED FOR any sounds of a disturbance and then peeked out the door. Parker headed for the medical center. She wasn't sure if he would get his ass kicked for this or not. But he had a good reason. Samson looked to be in good shape, but obviously they needed some food for him too. She had no choice but to sit here and wait.

She tossed her phone on her bed and stretched out. She wasn't prone for more than a minute when a knock came on the door. "Come in," she said.

The door opened, and Johnson walked in. Parker and Samson were not with him. He stopped, looking for Parker, then spun to look at her.

"He needed food and water for the dog," she said.

Johnson frowned for a long moment, as if processing the viability of the words, then gave a clipped nod. "I'll go check on him."

"You do that," she said.

Sandy reached for her bag and pulled it up on the bed. "Can I have a shower, or is it forbidden?"

Johnson stopped at the entrance and nodded. "Take it now."

She reached up and pinched the bridge of her nose. She hated this sensation of being a prisoner. Following orders was something she was used to but not like this.

"Why is it that I had to come here myself?" she asked herself, not for the first time. She could have stayed at home and waited for them to bring Jeremy back, but she'd felt she needed to come to escort him on his final trip. They'd been very close; it was the least she could do. She loved her brother dearly and couldn't believe his love of the navy was what had taken his life. She had no clue what she would do without him in her life.

As for her new career, she had options. Lots of them. She just didn't feel inclined to go in any one direction. And, right now, she wanted to get clean and have a good night's sleep and then try to put this very distressing day behind her. There was no thought of preparing for her terrible tomorrow. She only knew she had to get through it somehow. She grabbed her toiletries, her nightclothes and stepped outside.

The MP out front turned to look at her. "I'm going for a shower," she said.

He nodded and pointed in the direction. She took a deep breath to calm down, as she realized she and Parker were truly being guarded. Was it so they couldn't leave? No. Maybe not guarded, maybe protected? Not that somebody would come after them. Not a thought she wanted to consider but something that maybe she had to. If she wanted to look on the military police actions in a more favorable light, she'd have to consider that maybe they were trying to protect them.

She undressed in the locker area of the showers, stepped into the shower cubicle and blasted the water. The first shot of water was cold, and she shivered as she let out a teeny shriek. Once the water was warm, she tilted her head back and let the water run over her head and body. It was soothing, and she loved the feel of the water. She worked quickly, and, once she was done, wrapping herself up in a towel, she leaned here for a moment.

It would be the only time to herself that she had until she was back stateside. A disconcerting thought for somebody who normally lived a very private life. Finally she couldn't delay it any longer. After brushing her teeth, she dressed in the clothes she'd brought, wrapped a towel around her head, picked up the rest of her belongings and headed back. With any luck Parker would be there. She didn't like being alone here. Something deeply unsettling revolved about the day's events.

She hoped Parker had managed to get what they needed for Samson. He appeared to handle whatever was thrown at him with equal equanimity. She loved that about him. He deserved respect for his patience and his ability to deal, but, more than that, he had earned it. He had that air about him that stated who he was and, if you didn't like it, ... too bad. Not the same arrogance she'd seen in others but a sense of quiet power. As if he'd seen it all and knew he could handle it.

When he'd gone up that hill after the dog ... and came back, ... not only unharmed but with Samson, well, she'd been impressed. That he was calm even as they were being shot at said so much about him.

She walked into her new bunk and found Parker sitting on the side of his bed, with Samson in his crate nearby. Parker looked at her, surprised, then realized where she'd been and nodded in approval. "That's a really good idea. When I came in, and the place was empty, I wasn't sure what to think."

"I figured, if nothing else, it would get me a few minutes out of here," she said with half a smile. "I'm sure you saw the sentry."

He grinned at her. "Passive-aggressive bunch?"

She shook her head. "Right? But for me," she said, pulling back her blankets and curling up under them. Reaching up she rubbed the towel around her hair in an attempt dry it faster. "it's more a case of taking a moment of freedom while I'm allowed it. I don't know what tomorrow will bring. And I can't say this is what I thought I signed up for."

"Agreed," Parker said, standing up with his own bag. "Let's hope tomorrow is better. I'll go for a shower myself. Are you okay here with Samson?"

She glanced over to see Samson sleeping in his crate, out for the night. "We'll do just fine," she said. "Don't wake me when you come back."

"I won't," he said. He left quietly. In spite of herself and in spite of all that had happened, she closed her eyes and fell asleep.

WHEN PARKER RETURNED to his barracks, he wasn't surprised to find her sleeping. Too many emotional situations for both of them had happened today, and tomorrow would likely be much worse. Samson appeared to be out for the count too. Even in his crate, he'd stretched out on his side, his legs straight out in front, with light snores accompanying the rise and fall of his chest. Now if only Parker could do the same. But his mind spun endlessly on what had happened. And why ...

Something else seemed to be going on here, and he knew that, but, being on the way out and not belonging to the base anymore, he really had no options to get more information.

It kind of sucked. He didn't know how big the theft-of-government-property issue was, since the colonel already seemed aware of it, even working on it. Right? Were he and Sandy in any kind of danger? That was the last thing he wanted. Because of him, she had gone on that ride in the first place. Of course Badger and Commander Cross were likely to feel fairly guilty over all this as well. Or would if things went south. Right now they were all watching the proceedings with a wary eye.

He looked down at Samson, who lifted his head and looked back at him. "It's okay, boy."

Samson's ears twitched, but he never made a sound as he lay back down.

Parker pulled the covers up over his shoulders. Everything was so out of sync. This was already an emotional trip with his brother lying cold in the navy morgue. To think that, when Parker got home, he had to go through the whole funeral process and deal with his father was just another massive emotional roller coaster ride coming. But to have this added altercation happen while he was here paying his respects on the base where his brother had died? ... Well, that was even more upsetting.

He lay quietly, zoning in and out of sleep, knowing he needed to sleep but unable to. It seemed like he should have found something important amid all this, and yet he couldn't grasp what it might have been. As he lay here deep in thought, Samson raised the alarm.

He started with a growl, low, deep and barely discernible. But Parker heard it. He reached out a hand and touched Samson's paw against the cage. With Parker's eyes open, he adjusted to the darkness. He checked his watch; it was just after midnight.

He lay still as he searched for whatever was bothering Samson. The dog shifted in his crate, rolling onto his side and then up. He stood tall and turned to face the other side, where Sandy was. Parker bolted up and saw her form curled under the blanket still. He sighed with relief. "She's still there, buddy. It's okay."

But his whisper was so soft. And that's when he realized the movement on the other side of her bed, on the other side of the wall. This was one of the temporary barracks, not something they kept here for months on end. These structures came and went, depending on the numbers and the space required and didn't offer much beside protection from the elements.

He wouldn't have been at all surprised that they had thrown it up just for him and Sandy. There were windows, but they had plastic over the edges. He saw a figure outside who dropped down below the window and then straightened again, the shadow blending in with the moonlight. He watched it cross to the next window, drop under again and then come up around the back. It kept moving around their barracks and then sliding up on his side.

Not the actions of an appointed sentry on guard.

Samson once again growled, his gaze tracking the shadow as it went. "Right. Good call. Not sure who that is," Parker whispered. He straightened up, walked to the next window and watched the shadow approach. Parker peered outside.

Again not the appointed sentry doing a walk around the perimeter on a regular time schedule since the figure never went past this particular corner of the barracks. He watched and waited, but the guy stayed behind that corner. Close to

Samson and close to Parker's bed. And that made Parker angry.

He opened the door just enough of a crack to see the moonlight, with enough light that he could see any shadows shifting. All clear. Parker let the door drift open enough to step out. Still moving silently, barefoot, he crept closer to the corner where the intruder should have been. And then he heard the breathing. Whoever it was still stood on the other side, just out of sight. Parker waited. He should have brought Samson with him, except the dog probably would have growled and given away their position.

Whoever was standing there hopefully didn't know Parker was here. Then he heard a voice around the corner.

"They're sleeping," said the terse male voice.

Parker couldn't hear the response when it came back, but the watcher answered, "The dog's there too."

A moment of silence ensued.

"I can do that."

More silence.

"I said, I can do it." The phone call ended with a growl.

Parker watched the shadows as the intruder pulled out a handgun and put a silencer on the end. Parker stepped quickly back toward the open door. Inside the entrance of the doorway just a few steps away from the gunman, he watched as a man in a military police uniform crept toward the open door. As soon as the handgun swept up and pointed at Sandy, Parker grabbed it and drop-kicked the MP to the ground. He twisted his arm back and around and held him down, hitting a pressure point to knock him out.

Moving as quietly as he could, he dragged the man back inside.

"What did you do?" Sandy asked from behind him.

"Stopped him from shooting you," he said.

"I saw him," she said. "I heard a noise and bolted up, and that's when I saw the damn gun."

"Yeah," Parker said, his voice harsh but very low. "We've been targeted."

With the man on the ground in front of Parker, his knee pressed in the MP's back, he quickly sent Badger a text message. It seemed stupid to be contacting Badger, but right now Parker didn't know who else to trust. Badger's response was **On it.**

He almost laughed. Sent him a reply. **Faster than that please.**

He didn't get a response, and he didn't expect one. Ten minutes later a march of boots came toward him. He held up his finger to Sandy.

She nodded.

Samson growled. Parker walked over and released the hatch on the cage and brought Samson to stand guard over the man down.

At the door, there was a knock.

"Who is it?" Parker asked, his voice hard.

"Colonel Barek," he said. "I spoke to you earlier tonight."

"You did," Parker replied.

"I want to come in," the colonel said.

"That's nice. Are you coming in alone? With or without weapons?" Parker asked. He now held his would-be assailant's gun in his hand.

"Young man, I think you're in a bit over your head," the colonel's voice said calmly.

"And I think you've lost control of your base," Parker said, his voice equally soft.

There was a sucked-in breath, and the door slammed open. The colonel stepped in and slammed the door behind him. He stared at Parker intently, every line of his body was taut.

Parker stood his ground. He motioned at the man on the ground. "He came in to shoot us, not fifteen minutes ago. This is his weapon, and it was pointed directly at Sandy. I heard him outside talking to somebody on his phone about *taking care of it.*"

The colonel looked down at the man, frowned, turned to Parker. "That explains why Commander Cross contacted me in the middle of the night."

"Unless you wanted to discuss cake recipes, I would presume so," Parker snapped.

He heard Sandy's gasp. She walked over and faced the colonel. "The door opened, and I saw this man holding a gun in my direction. I didn't have time to react, just rolled sideways, and Parker reached up and subdued him."

The colonel's shoulders sagged ever-so-slightly. "Damn it," he said. "We thought we had this dealt with."

"I presume you still have somebody double-crossing you within the base."

The colonel looked at him and gave a brief smile. "Something like that. Nothing quite so Hollywoodish."

"Betrayal comes in many forms," Sandy said. "It doesn't have to be Hollywood style at all. It just has to be somebody who's looking to profit from their own actions instead of helping our country."

"And again, something like that," he said. "But you appear to have stirred up a hornet's nest by finding Ronnie."

"Ronnie or the dog?"

The colonel glanced at Samson, glanced at the cage and

saw the open door.

"I let him out for our own defense," Parker said coolly. "He's the one that alerted me to our current mess."

The colonel nodded. "These dogs have saved many lives," he said. He lifted his hat from his head and ran his fingers through his hair. "So we have one MP who's a bad egg," he said. "Now the question is, how many others are there?"

"Do you recognize him, sir?" Sandy asked. "Or is there a chance the real MP is tied up or dead somewhere else and missing his uniform?"

The colonel's gaze went from her to Parker and nodded slowly. "As much as I wish that were the case, I do recognize him. Now we have a bigger problem." He opened the door and called for two men. Both of them, senior aides, came in and took one look. Their faces dropped. They reached down and grabbed the prisoner, had a quick discussion in low tones that neither Parker nor Sandy could hear. They escorted the man away. The colonel looked at the handgun in Parker's hand and said, "Son, I need that."

"I'm sure you do," Parker said, staring down at it. "The problem is, we're the ones now caught in the middle of something we had no involvement in. And we don't have weapons."

"You shouldn't need them here."

"But obviously we do," Sandy said, her hand rubbing the top of Samson's head and linking her arm through Parker's. "Can't say either of us feel very safe here now."

Parker turned the handgun away from his body and held it out handle first to the colonel. "We are more than happy to leave this base," he said.

The colonel nodded slowly. "I'll change the sentries and

put two men on guard," he said. "They won't be MPs. They'll be my own men. Get some sleep. You'll need it. Tomorrow is an emotional day for you both." He turned, glanced back at Samson, and said, "And, if he's not in that cage, he needs to be. Do you hear me?"

"I hear you," Parker said. "But I also want to remind you that he's the one that saved our lives."

"Noted," the colonel said. "You know how much paperwork this will entail now?" He turned and took his leave.

When the door clanged behind him, an almost palpable change came in the air.

Sandy glanced at Parker. "Okay, that was rough too."

"Go ahead and sleep," he said.

She snorted. "I don't think I'll be able to."

"I know," he said. "It's almost one in the morning. Not even sure how that came to take so long. But we have to get up at six a.m., so we have five hours. Trying to stay awake is almost impossible too."

She remained where she was and asked, "What do you think about all this?"

"I'm afraid we disturbed somebody when we spoke to Ronnie, and I think someone is afraid that we might have seen them or something."

"Did you tell the colonel about those two men, Gorman and Tobey, present when Samson disappeared?"

Parker shook his head. "No, I don't think I did."

She nodded. "Maybe he needs to be updated." Parker stared down at his phone, and she said, "Personally I'd probably text him the same way that you got him to come here. It's got to be easier than facing the guards out there."

He chuckled. "I'm sending the information to Badger, asking him to relay it to the colonel. But I also need to update Badger on this shooter now too."

Sandy waved her hand at him. Then walked closer and gave him a quick hug. "You do that. I'm done. I'm going back to sleep."

"I thought you couldn't sleep," he said teasingly, hating to see her step away from him. She'd felt so right in his arms, even if for only a moment.

"Sure, but the alternative sucks too. So I'll try."

He watched as she pulled out a set of headphones, popped them into her ears and pulled the blankets around her.

He smiled, settled back, and texted Badger. It would be a long night. The colonel might have put good people in charge out front of their barracks, but Parker wouldn't take a chance. He had trusted somebody already tonight to look after them, and that obviously hadn't gone well. He wouldn't make that same mistake twice.

CHAPTER 6

I N SPITE OF herself, she slept. When she awoke again, she bolted upright, grabbing for the side of the bed.

"Take it easy," Parker said. "It's okay."

She glanced at him, then sighed with relief as she remembered where she was. She sagged against the pillow as she rubbed her face. When she refocused, she saw Parker sitting up, leaning against the back of the bed, with Samson also stretched out on Parker's bed, half on top of him.

"I see you and Samson are bonding," she said in a light tone before a yawn overtook her.

Samson lifted his head and gave a bark. His tail wagged as he watched her.

"He's a great dog," Parker said. "A part of me says I should take him home myself and keep him."

"If you want him, you know you could probably have him," she said. "He needs a good home after what he's been through. And you do have an in with the military. Not to mention, Samson trusts you."

He stroked Samson gently. "I would like to keep him."

"Either you or me. He's the last link we have to our brothers," she murmured, staring at Parker and Samson, loving the connection between man and dog. They had a bond already. She couldn't imagine separating them and the further stress that would bring to Samson. For Parker it might not be as bad, but the longer the two were together, the harder it would be. Parker looked like an all-or-nothing type of guy. She'd listened to her brother talk about Jerry's family, and Parker had been mentioned, always with respect and fondness.

She was grateful he was here with her. This was a crap trip in the first place. Adding that to everything that had happened since they'd first arrived, well, ... it didn't bear thinking about being alone right now. Plus she really liked Parker. Wanted to spend time with him. It would be lovely to stay in touch when back stateside. And not just for the connection with their brothers …

"But is that a good enough reason?" he asked. "Or should we be looking at what's best for him?"

"Meaning, neither of us have a job in a couple weeks and have no clue where and how we'll be, so do we have any business keeping a dog like that?"

He chuckled. "All of that and more, yes."

"The thing is, if you make him a priority," Sandy said, "other things will fall in line."

"Right," Parker said. "Something to think about. And, speaking of which, it's almost six, and this guy needs to go outside." He patted Samson on the back. "Do you want to go out, Samson?"

Samson barked and jumped off Parker's bed, gave an excited yelp and stretched out his front paws.

"I'm coming with you then," Sandy said. "I don't want to be left alone anymore." She hesitated, looked at her bag, and asked, "Could you turn your back for a second?"

"Or do you want us to walk you to the bathroom?"

She nodded and smiled. "I have to go anyway, so, if we can do that, that would be great."

Samson walked over to Sandy, his tail wagging ferociously. His body wiggled with joy, as if saying good morning.

She crouched in front of him and hugged him gently. "Thank you for saving my life, big guy."

He nudged her for more attention, which she willingly gave him. When she could stand again, she slipped on her shoes and grabbed her bag, and the three of them went to the women's bathroom. She changed, brushed her teeth, her hair and washed her face. Her eyes were still gritty from lack of sleep, but she felt much better and more prepared for the day. The only trick now was to get through today and to get home.

Maybe then some sense of normalcy would come again. Although not likely. Did one ever get over losing a sibling?

Nor could she get over the feeling of being disconnected from everything around her. She was still in the service, but it didn't feel like it was her world anymore. She was in a transition from this to … what? When she stepped back out, Samson greeted her with a wagging tail, and Parker had a smile on his face. She grinned at the two of them, loving that they were waiting for her. She motioned to her bag.

He nodded. "Let's go back and put it in with mine."

She realized he was fully dressed. "Lucky you," she said. "I gather you got dressed while I was sleeping."

"Yep," he said cheerfully. "I didn't mind if you looked."

That got a laugh out of her. "Now if I'd only realized that," she said, "I would have had sweet dreams instead of holding nightmares at bay."

He squeezed her hand gently. "It was a pretty tough night," he said. "I'm glad you got some sleep."

"I did," she said. "But I'll be feeling the shortness of it by the time we get on the plane today."

"Both of us," he said. "Let's just try to get through the day together. Being together will help. And, with any luck, there won't be any delays, and we'll be soon on our way home."

"Do you think that's possible?" she asked in a low tone, glancing around. "I have to admit I've been worried about that. With this nightmare they could hold us here for days, weeks even."

"It's possible," he said with a nod. "Hopefully not that long though."

She gripped his fingers hard. "I feel like I've already been here too long. Let's pray it goes smoothly."

He hadn't let her hand go. And she hadn't let his go either. As if, in these circumstances, they were clinging to each other for support. She kind of liked it. But then she liked him. "Our brothers were good friends. You know that, right?"

"Of course," he said. "I heard about you a lot from mine. All good things."

"I know the military was the making of Jeremy," she said. "He'd always been insecure and full of self-doubt and worried about his future. But he stepped up and stepped in and never looked back."

"I think, like Jerry, it was their lives here. It made them who they were," Parker said. "In a way, I don't think they would have minded that they died in the line of fire."

"No. I know Jeremy already told me that he'd be happy to die in action," she said. "It makes me sad. Because it's almost like he put that thought out there, and the world gave it to him. I don't want to even think about something like that being possible."

"I think it's a simple case that they were following what was true to their hearts. They lived well, and they died even better," he said. "We have to give them whatever honor we can for doing that. We're the ones left behind, trying to live without them, and yet in this mess still surrounding us. It's up to us to make the best of it and to get home and to carry on."

"True," she said. "But somehow it doesn't feel like it'll be anywhere near that simple."

He chuckled. "Nothing in the military is ever simple."

"Yet it should be," she argued. "With all the layers of brass and checks and balances, everything should be cut and dry."

"The minute you add people into the mix, nothing is simple. Remember that. Just because it all looks like it's being taken care of, doesn't mean it is."

"I only have to look at the way you're communicating to understand that. You're contacting somebody outside of the military to contact somebody in the military to contact somebody here on base."

"Because we can't take a chance. We've already flushed out one person who didn't have our best interests at heart, and that means, after they check that MP's phone, they should find several more."

"That's a disturbing thought too," Sandy said. "We really don't have a clue. Anybody on this base could be part of this."

"I know," Parker said. "So just stay calm, stay focused, and we'll get through this. Together."

He motioned at their barracks. "Let's drop off our bags and go get some breakfast."

"Agreed," she said. "But, at the same time, I'm hoping

you'll stick close. I don't want to end up being separated, not knowing what happened to you. After one attempt on our lives, the minute you're not here at my side, I'll assume somebody got you."

"Ditto," he said with a smile. "You stay close to me, and I'll stay close to you."

PARKER KEPT AN eye out as they headed for the mess hall. Sandy glanced at him. "No guards today?"

He nodded his chin slightly to the left and said in a low voice, "They're keeping an eye on us. Don't you worry. They are just a little harder to see."

"That's kind of creepy." She slipped her arm through his, stepping that much closer.

He looked down at their joined arms and smiled. "You can do that anytime you want," he said.

She flashed a smile back at him. "I'm sure you have a dozen girlfriends back home," she teased. "I don't want to step on any toes."

He pressed her arm against his body and chuckled. "Nope. No girlfriend. At least not right now. Not in the last six months actually," he said thoughtfully as they continued to the mess hall.

"Wow. A cutie like you? I don't believe it."

"Same for you," he said. "What's a pretty girl like you doing over here?"

"Well, I wish it wasn't for the reason that we're both here," she said, the humor falling away. She stopped a few feet from the mess hall tent and looked at Samson. "We're not allowed to take him inside."

Parker nodded. "I'm not leaving him alone either," he said, his voice steady. He glanced around. "You go in first and get yourself something to eat. I'll wait here with Samson."

She frowned and shook her head, then gripped his arm tighter. "No. I don't want to separate. What if we both went in and took the dog to the far side?"

"Not sure that'll work either," he said in a joking manner.

She looked at her watch. "We are still early. We could just walk through, and, if somebody doesn't like it, they'll stop us."

He cocked an eyebrow at her and smiled. "All they can do is tell us to take him out."

They proceeded into the mess hall tent, picked up trays, then plates, and served themselves a hefty breakfast. They didn't waste any time, moving from one end to the other, poured coffee and proceeded to the far side of the tent by one of the back openings. They sat down with Samson beside them.

"We should have stopped to get him some food," she stated quietly.

"We'll go to the supply department and see if we can get him breakfast," Parker said. "Otherwise, gee, poor Samson will have to have a sausage or two."

"I think poor Samson would prefer sausages," Sandy said with a laugh. "But he needs more than a couple."

The two of them sat with their backs to the bulk of the people coming through now and kept to themselves, while they quickly ate their breakfast undisturbed. Sandy left a sausage on her plate.

Parker looked at it, raised his gaze to her and smiled.

"Samson?" He reached out a hand and gave it to the dog. It disappeared in two seconds. And Samson looked at them with adoring chocolate eyes, his ears up, as if looking for more.

She reached down and hugged him.

"Maybe I should go get him some more sausages?" Without letting Parker answer, Sandy got up from the table and took her plate back to the food buffet, grabbing more sausages and bacon. On her way back, she snagged some cheese as well.

Parker laughed.

She shrugged. "We don't want to be separated from him when he needs to eat," she said in a low whisper.

Parker removed the sausage from her plate to Samson's eager mouth. Halfway through feeding him the sausages, he shook his head. "We might be getting company."

"Time to leave?" she asked, her back stiffening, but she didn't turn around.

"It's hard to say." He picked up another sausage, took a bite and handed it to Samson.

When the two men who had entered the mess were halfway toward them, Parker gave Samson the last two bites and stood. "Let's go to the supply office and see if we can get him some dog food."

She chuckled. "Like he'll want that now."

Parker exited the back of the tent with the dog, and Sandy cleaned up their dishes and followed.

As they stood outside, Parker motioned with his hand and said, "Let's head this way." Almost like he wanted to avoid the men.

"Are you trying to lose them?" she asked.

"Not deliberately, no. But I didn't really want to talk to

the two who came into the tent."

"Who were they?"

"Two of the MPS from last night."

"Oh," Sandy said with a nod. "I don't want anything to do with them either."

At the supply office, Parker stepped in and asked if he could get some dog food.

The clerk behind the desk looked at him and said, "Paperwork?"

He sighed. "Nope. Same answer as last night. We weren't supposed to be here. The dog was not supposed to be here. We are leaving today, but the dog can't suffer."

The clerk frowned at him and said, "I need paperwork."

"Okay, so you tell me how am I supposed to feed this dog before he flies out this afternoon?"

The clerk looked at him, gave him a bland smile, and said, "I suggest you go to the mess hall tent."

"You don't even have any free samples left that Samson could have?"

At that, the clerk frowned, as if Parker's words had nudged something. "I might have something. Hang on." He disappeared into the back, came out with a small six-inch-size bag. "This is the best I can do."

Parker took it and nodded to him. "Thanks." Trying hard to keep his voice from being too curt, he stepped out of the office. He held it up for Sandy to see.

She frowned. "Not very generous for a dog his size, are they?"

"Considering that he just ate sausages, it might hold him for a bit. Let's get him back and see if we can feed him this."

Still not stopped by anybody—but constantly under watch because Parker could feel their gazes on him—he led the way back to their accommodations.

As soon as they were inside, Sandy walked over to their stuff and said, "Okay. Doesn't look like anybody touched our bags."

"Were you expecting that?" Parker asked curiously. He sat down on the bed, ripped open the package and offered the kibbles to Samson.

Samson looked at him as if to say, *Are you nuts?*

"Sorry, bud, but this is all they gave me."

Samson grudgingly took a few from his hand, then stopped, spit them out. Parker put the bag in his pocket and said, "We'll use the kibble later, if we need to."

Samson didn't look impressed with that idea either.

Sandy hopped up and said, "Let me get him some water. I'll see if there's a container in the shower room." She headed out of their room to the women's showers.

Parker didn't know what she would use for a container but was happy to leave it with her. He settled back on the bed, wondering what the day would bring. There would be a small ceremony at noon, and then they would be escorted back to the airfield and hopefully fly home without any more problems.

He gently stroked Samson. "What will we do with you, buddy?"

But Samson stared at the doorway where Sandy had left. When the hairs on the back of his neck stood up, Parker shot to his feet and raced to the door.

He bent down to Samson and said, "Where is she, boy? Where is she?"

He gave Samson just enough of a lead that he could follow. Samson bolted for the women's washroom. As if he knew that was where she'd gone. Parker had enough trust in

Samson's nose to follow.

As they reached the washroom, a woman came out. He stopped her and asked if Sandy was in there. The woman looked at him, shook her head, and said, "No, it's empty." And she walked away.

Under his breath he whispered, "Shit." He shook Samson's lead slightly. "Find her, boy."

Samson started to run. Trying to make it look like Parker was out for a jog, he followed along, hoping to not raise any alarms.

But the alarm in his head was already sounding out loud and clear. She was gone, and he had no clue why or where, but she wouldn't have left without him if she had had a choice. Which meant somebody had stopped her on her way to or from the shower.

The dog kept heading away from their quarters, along the fence line to a building in the back. There Samson stopped and sat down. Parker slowly approached, looking in through a window.

She was, indeed, there, and two men stood over her. She sat with her arms crossed, glaring up at them. As he stepped back, he heard her say, "Where's Parker?"

"What's your association with Parker?" one of the men asked.

Shifting his angle, Parker could see they were the same two MPs in the mess hall earlier. Frowning, he sent Badger a message, how the two MPs took Sandy away to a nondescript building. He didn't get an immediate response, but he stood to the side and listened in on the conversation.

"He's the brother of my brother's friend," she said. "I don't know him well, only spent a little time with him since we both arrived here to bring our brothers home. Both kind of on an emotional journey that is difficult enough," she said. "Why? Why don't you ask him questions?"

"We would if we could," one of them replied, "but he wasn't in the barracks."

"I doubt he's gone far," Sandy said. "I just went to get a water dish for the dog."

"And yet you were in the shower room?"

"I was looking for water but also hoping I could find something to put water in for Samson," she explained.

Parker could hear the frustration in her voice.

"We wanted to ask you questions about what happened at the airport hangar," the one said.

"If you were doing that officially," she said, "you would have taken me back to your office. Not lead me to a far building on the base where I am now isolated and separated from everyone. I'm still military personnel, you know?"

"Do you think that'll make a difference?" the other man said with a sneer.

At that Samson growled low and deep in the back of his throat. Parker placed a hand on his head, hoping to quiet him. It was obvious Samson didn't like the man's tone of voice.

One of the men asked, "What was that?"

"Likely nothing," she said. "It'll be your imagination, just like all the rest of this is."

"What are you talking about?"

"You're looking for me to provide dirt on Parker. He didn't do anything. I didn't do anything. We're both innocent."

"That's what they all say," he said.

"Are you guys even sure you're MPs? I'd like to see your IDs."

"Oh, sorry. I left it back at the base. We're the ones asking the questions," he snapped.

"Meaning, you refuse to identify yourselves?"

Parker could almost see Sandy make a mental note; then she gave a clipped nod. "I'll be sure to let somebody else know about that. There is a proper procedure to follow."

Just then Parker's phone vibrated. He checked it out to see Badger's response. **You got company coming.**

He stepped off to the side, so he could see who it was. And, sure enough, the colonel's two personal men appeared, those assigned to them earlier.

As soon as they saw him, he walked toward them.

In a low voice they asked, "What's going on?"

He pointed to the building. "She went to get water for Samson from the showers, and those two MPs directed her down here. They've refused to identify themselves and are asking her questions about the airport. And me," he said succinctly.

The men nodded and warned him, "You stay here."

They walked into the building as he watched. When they stepped out a moment later, they frowned at him. "It's empty."

CHAPTER 7

S HE COULDN'T BELIEVE she was being hustled out the back and around to another area of the compound. She'd been picked up by the elbows and rushed out, all the while being ordered to stay silent. That she was in trouble was obvious. Why had she left to get water alone? Where was Parker? Surely he had noticed she was missing already.

"What are you doing?" she demanded.

One of the men glared at her and said, "One more word out of you, and you won't be able to talk again."

She struggled to free herself. "Let me go."

A hard blow hit her across the face. She crumpled into their grips, momentarily stunned from the blow. Her feet now dragging along the ground were lifted, and they fully carried her until she was dumped on a cot, and both men stood guard beside her.

She glared up at them. "This is completely unacceptable."

"You don't know the half of it," one snapped. The two men checked their watches.

She rubbed her swollen cheek and struggled to sit up. "You just kidnapped me. You know you'll get in trouble for this."

A part of her kept telling herself to shut her mouth because she was aggravating them. Not to mention the fact that dead women left no tales, whereas, if they left her alive, she'd be telling everything she knew.

In the distance she heard a shout and then sounds of running feet. She glared up at them. "When they find me," she said, "you have no idea how wrong this will go for you."

The two men looked at each other and, within seconds, raced outside and disappeared. She hopped to her feet and ran out. Just as she came around the corner, she was scooped up. She struggled to fight, only to hear Parker's voice, "It's okay, Sandy. It's all right. It's me."

When she realized it was him, she turned, threw her arms around his neck and hung on tight. He held her close from hip to chest. She could feel his heart slamming against his chest, … or was that hers? Then she heard him whispering, "Thank God, we found you."

And realized it had been both of their hearts slamming in fear.

Samson whined. Still in Parker's embrace, Sandy reached out a hand, and Samson thrust his nose into her palm. She gently stroked him as she hung on to Parker. When she could, she whispered, "Didn't we promise we wouldn't get separated?"

"Yeah. Then you went to get water for the dog. Who knew somebody would kidnap you?"

She wanted to cry, but, at the same time, she didn't want to. Still too much anger kept her spine stiff and rigid, while fear kept her arms locked around Parker. When she could, she relaxed her grip and leaned back to smile up at him.

But his smile fell away when he saw her face. He turned her head to the side and bit off, "Which one of those two assholes did that to you?"

Her eyebrows shot up. "Did you see them with me?"

He nodded. "And, against my better judgment, I didn't race in because I wasn't sure if they were armed," he said. "I was waiting for these two guys to arrive. Big mistake. When they finally entered, you were gone."

"They must have heard something or got a signal of some kind. Because, all of a sudden, they picked me up and pulled me out the back. Next thing I knew, they were half dragging me around the corner." She pointed to where she had just come from. "It wasn't far, but it was obviously another empty barracks. Somewhere along the way, when I started to fight back, one of them smacked me hard." She reached up to touch her puffy cheek and winced. "That won't look pretty."

"You'll always be beautiful," Parker said, gently kissing her on the nose. "That's for the *owie*. And a puffy cheek won't change that. But I'll get my hands on that asshole. You can count on it." His tone was low and ominous.

One of the colonel's men stepped forward and said, "Not your problem."

Parker glared at him. "If you guys can't do your damn jobs, somebody else has to step in, and, in this case, that asshole won't get away with hitting her."

One soldier stepped forward. "I'm Sergeant Hall. This is Paulson." He reached out a hand and gripped Parker on the shoulder. "We will take care of this. Trust us."

Parker snorted. "Trust? I had to get help through a backhand request."

They nodded and shrugged.

"The two men will have ditched the uniforms by now," Hall said. "Can you give us something descriptive to identify them?"

"One was tall, reddish hair," Sandy said. "More Slaviclooking, high cheekbones but real thin. The second guy had an olive skin tone, black hair, heavyset, more of a gut. I didn't see much of his features except for the nose. It was broken. A big bulbous nose. Very odd looking."

Hall said, "We might know him. We'll update the colonel and see about tracking these two down. The colonel will want you to personally identify these men."

"Or let us stay some place nice and public and run a group of men past us, and we'll pick them out," Parker said quietly. "The last thing you want is to have us locked up in the colonel's office."

Paulson and Hall frowned.

"We are not planning on being separated again," Sandy said, looping her arm with Parker's, Samson standing between them. "How foolish that last attack was. All I wanted to do was get the dog a drink. We can't even get dog food because everybody here needs paperwork for this poor animal to get a meal."

Hall looked down at the dog. "They wanted paperwork to authorize the release of dog food? Of course they did."

"I do want another coffee," Sandy said, almost aggressively. "My face is starting to really hurt."

The men nodded. "Do you want to go to medical first?"

"I'm a nurse. I can take care of this myself. But it's starting to sting. And I'm tired and fed up." She pulled Parker with her. "And you won't let me go. Will you?"

"No," Parker replied. He slid his hand down to her hand and clasped it tightly, raising his hand so she could see their interlocked fingers. "This is where you stay. And, by the way, you have Samson to thank for that distraction that sent the men running."

She glanced at Parker in surprise and then down at Samson. She crouched and wrapped her now freed hand around the dog and gave him a big cuddle. "Thanks for finding me, Samson," she said. "I don't know what those two men were up to, and I don't know what they would have done if you hadn't sent out the alarm so fast."

"Which direction did they go?" Hall asked.

She pointed to the left. "There, but then who knows where they ended up," Sandy said.

"Did any of the questions they asked give you any idea what they were looking for?"

"Just questions about Parker. Questions about the airport. Almost normal questions, as if they were military police investigating a case. But they weren't asking properly. Not like they were official. They wouldn't show me any IDs. Not to mention, they hit me and transferred me to another unofficial location."

She glanced at the two men as the four of them walked toward the mess hall. "I thought we had people on watch. Keeping an eye on us?"

Paulson nodded. "Exactly. And they were relieved by the two MPs who took you away."

"So they *were* military police?" she asked.

They shook their heads but didn't clearly answer. "That's what we'll check out."

She realized they were almost at the mess hall tent again. She let out a sigh of relief as they were seated at a big table outside toward the back, where they were out of the main traffic areas. Paulson and Hall then left them.

Parker sat right beside her and said, "We're up against a fine conundrum. I want to go in and get a coffee, but I've got Samson. And I don't want to leave you."

She thought about it and said, "We go together."

Just like that, the three stood and walked through the mess hall tent and headed straight for the coffee. Sandy also picked up several muffins, and they headed back outside.

When she sat back down, she said, "What did they want with me?"

"Answers," Parker said, stirring his coffee. "The question really is, why? And what did they think you would have to say?"

"I don't know anything," she replied. "Unless it goes back to all those photos I took at the hangar. Or did they assume that if I took a photo I'd seen something myself. Taking me out means no witness."

Parker looked at her. "Good point. Maybe we should check those out a little closer."

"It would be better to have my laptop," Sandy said with a half smile.

"It'll be hard to see either screen outside. We could take our coffee back to the mess tent, but ..."

"But we've been asked to stay here," she finished for him. "I have my phone. Let me take a look." She brought up the gallery of photos and flicked through them. "It's not like we'll see anything. A lot of detail is here. I need a big monitor to identify what we're looking at."

"One thought's been bugging me. And I wished to hell I'd checked it out while we were there. But it occurred to me later ... what if someone was hiding out in that hangar while we were there? They'd have been well hidden, but it's possible. I did a cursory search when we entered, but I wasn't expecting anyone to still be hanging around with a dead man there," Parker said in a low voice, leaning closer to study the images as she brought them up.

"Nobody attacked us," Parker continued, "but maybe

they didn't like the odds and didn't want to make their presence known. What are the chances that, when the MPs arrived, the hidden guy managed to change his hiding spot? Or one of the MPs was involved and helped him get away? Or alternatively he stayed hidden until everybody else left?"

"The trouble is, we can't know because we were the first to leave," Sandy said. "They could have hidden in there, or they could have gone out back and headed cross-country. It was dark. They could have gone anywhere at that time."

"I know," Parker said. "I was thinking of that. No other wheels were there either."

"It's not that far. It's only a couple miles from here on the same base. Hardly an issue for anyone with navy training."

"True." He tapped one of her pictures and asked, "See that doorway? Do you see something different there?"

She tried to expand the photo so they could see the details. "I'm not sure." She leaned in closer. "Is that a foot?"

"I'm thinking it's a boot," he said. "The question is, was there somebody inside that boot?"

They looked at each other and bent to look closer at her screen. "That would have been behind where the coats and coveralls were hung," she said finally.

"That makes sense that there would be spare boots there too. So we don't know for sure that what we're seeing is actually a person, as it could literally be a spare pair of boots."

Sandy frowned. "We did walk that area. So we would have noticed somebody."

"Would we have, really?" Parker asked thoughtfully. "We had a short amount of time to search. And quite a few pairs of overalls were there."

"They were bunched up, weren't they? Did we miss somebody in there? Did somebody hide while we were there, taking all those photos? And then, when the military police left, they snuck out?"

"They wouldn't need much time. Besides, if they had fooled us, chances are they fooled the military police who were there too. We left three MPs behind. Maybe one knew the guy was trying to hide, and maybe none of them had anything to do with it."

Sandy nodded, putting her phone down.

Parker picked it up. "May I?"

"Go ahead. Take a look," she replied. "I'm confused. I don't know what's going on anymore."

"I think what's going on is easy. Reselling US military goods. The problem is finding out who is behind it all."

"So we're talking about stolen goods from this base are then moved out to the private market?"

Parker nodded. "We already know Ronnie had to either know somebody or was involved. Or wanted to be involved or wasn't involved but wanted kickbacks to not involve anybody else. It's all conjecture on our part."

"We're still here for another few hours," Sandy said. "Can we do anything to narrow this down?"

Parker tapped another photo she had taken of the overalls, and, while she watched, he used his fingers to enlarge the photo. They both studied it when he tapped the top and asked, "Does that look like a nose to you?"

She peered into the photo, enlarging that one section until it blurred out. "I don't know," she said quietly. "It's a disconcerting thought to consider we might have missed somebody who was there and likely killed Ronnie."

"I know. We had time to capture him too."

"He was good though ..." She looked at Parker. "Samson was out of his cage. How is it he didn't know a man was there?"

Parker frowned. "That's the best argument we have yet as to that not being a person." He pondered some more. "Except Samson was lying almost always in front of that area, wasn't he?"

Sandy nodded. "He was. Which could mean he knew whoever was hiding there."

"Right. It could have been a game they played too. One of the things the dogs learn is to hunt out people in hiding."

"But surely Samson wouldn't have been taught to lay down at his feet?"

"Yes, that would have been part of his training," Parker said quietly. "Chances are though it was somebody he worked with all the time. There could have been a hand signal from the overalls we didn't see but which instructed Samson to lie down and relax."

"Scary thought. To think Samson already had so much information, and we never even asked him." She snickered.

"Because we don't speak the same language," Parker replied with a laugh. He reached down to pet Samson, who was eyeing the muffin on the table. "Do you think he's hungry?"

"He's a dog," Sandy said. "Dogs eat anytime, anything, anywhere."

"So true." Parker tossed the muffin to Samson and then chuckled, only to look back down at the photos, his smile falling away. "If someone was hidden in the hangar, Samson was just lying there, completely relaxed, because he knew perfectly well who was there and respected him. And, if that's the case, ... how do we get him to tell us who it was that he was doing that with?"

"Another trainer maybe?"

His gaze lit up. "That's not a bad idea. But what we need is somebody on our side who will find the right people to talk to."

"I don't imagine too many K9 trainers are here, but what if there were only a half dozen? You'd have the same problem of possibly talking to the wrong one." They drank their coffee until Sandy asked, "What happened to Samson's handler?"

"I'm not sure. I assumed he was badly injured in the same accident that finished Samson's career."

"But what if he wasn't? Who do we know who would have worked with the dogs? Surely if we had all the K9 handlers here, Samson would show us which ones he was comfortable with."

"He's most likely comfortable with all of them. I don't know how many are here at any point in time but maybe well over thirty or forty."

"Maybe the colonel can tell us?"

Parker pulled out his phone, and she grinned. "You'll contact Badger again?"

He chuckled. "The colonel hasn't given me his direct contact information and neither have the two men who brought us here."

Just then a shadow fell over Parker's shoulder. He looked up, and there were Sergeants Hall and Paulson, standing behind them, watching Parker.

Sergeant Hall squatted beside him and asked in a low voice, "Who are you texting?" Parker gave him a flat stare, and the man shrugged. "The colonel said you can talk to him directly."

"He didn't give us any contact information though, did he?" Parker said, also in an equally low tone.

Hall hesitated, then nodded. "Do you have something to send to him?"

"Any chance of getting him on the end of a phone? Or at least running a couple ideas past him?"

The soldier checked his watch and said, "He'll be back in his office in a few minutes. Let's go for a walk."

They stood. Sandy pocketed the rest of the muffins, while Parker wrapped Samson's rope around his hand, and they headed for the colonel's office.

Hall left them outside, while he stepped in and then pulled open the door for them to enter.

Colonel Barek motioned at two seats. "So what's this about? I assumed it was over, since I was not getting any more phone calls from Commander Cross. I like the man just fine, but I don't like him involved in my business."

"Understood," Parker said. "The only problem for us is that we don't know who we're supposed to trust." His voice must have changed tone as Samson nuzzled his hand. "It's okay, boy," he whispered.

"Since I'm at the top of the food chain, you better start trusting me," the colonel said.

"When we were at the airport hangar with the dead body," Parker said, "we took a mess of photos. Now, while having coffee, we looked through a bunch of those that Sandy had taken. A few raise interesting questions."

"What photos?" the colonel barked.

Sandy held up her cell phone. He held out his hand, and she handed it over. He grabbed a USB cord and connected her phone to his laptop. "Come around here. What photos in particular?"

He swiped through the photos, his gaze stopping at the photo of Ronnie lying dead. "A good man," he said in a hard voice.

When the image came up that first caught Parker's attention, he called out, "Stop."

The colonel went back one and asked, "What am I looking at?"

"We were wondering if that pair of boots was attached to a human," Parker said.

They looked at it as largely as they could, and the commander said, "No way to know. Even if they were, what would that tell you?"

"That somebody was hiding among all those hanging clothes," Sandy said quietly. "If you swipe three more photos forward ..."

He flicked forward and stopped on one that appeared to be of the coats and hats.

Parker leaned forward and pointed at what he had thought was a face. "Is that a nose and eyes?"

The colonel stared at it for a long moment and then sat back. "Well, I'll be."

Two photos later, she had photos of Samson lying in front of the clothing. The colonel motioned at the dog. "So why wouldn't the dog have alerted you to his presence?"

Parker looked at him and said, "He did."

The colonel raised an eyebrow. "Explain."

"He was lying down in front of somebody he knew," Parker said. "As close as I can figure, he probably sniffed out the person, got a hand signal to lay down, calm and happy, thinking this was all part of his training."

"Which would mean somebody who the dog knew and who the dog trusted but also somebody who understood hand signals," the colonel said, speaking slowly.

Parker gave a clipped nod.

"Interesting theory and definitely a place to start." He looked at Samson and said, "Maybe he isn't leaving today."

"How many handlers do you have on base now?" Parker asked.

"Not many. I had seven who shipped out two days ago, before Ronnie was killed. I have six out in the field right now. I think I have five on base."

"Handlers or dogs?" Sandy asked, walking slowly around to sit back down on the chair in front of the desk. "Because a handler without a dog could still be somebody Samson knows well."

He nodded. "Good point." He called for Sergeant Hall to come back in. When the man stepped in, the colonel explained he wanted all the K9s' handlers, past and present, standing in his office within fifteen minutes. He then looked at Parker and asked, "Can you handle Samson? I want him kept out of sight until we get to the point of taking a look at the men."

Parker nodded. "I'll take him away and then bring him back in, once you've got everybody assembled. I'm still not sure how to have him show us who he knows and who he doesn't."

"I'll have to think about that. I used to do a bunch of K9 work myself way back when, but I haven't had to bring those skills into play in a long time."

Parker said, "And don't forget Sandy was kidnapped by two of your MPs."

"Not MPs. We found two military police officers trussed up in the back room of the station. They had been knocked out from behind and stripped. Both men will be okay, but they're pretty pissed themselves."

Sandy let out a long, hard breath. "That makes more sense. I was hoping they weren't actual MPs because, of course, that would just make this whole in-house situation worse."

"Exactly," the colonel said. "We still have to find the two men who attacked them and you."

"One of the men had a very distinctive face," Parker spoke up again. "Your Sergeant Hall thought he might have an idea who one of Sandy's kidnappers were, but Hall didn't give us a name. Said he would go find him."

"Good," the colonel said. "Because the last thing I want is this to go any further. I want everybody caught and thrown in the brig."

"I agree with that," Parker said. "We have two hours until the ceremony."

The colonel nodded, his face turning solemn. "Six men have died in the last week. Six men who shouldn't have. They gave their lives for this country, and here we have other men stealing from the very budget trying to help protect our men."

"There's no reasoning with some people," Parker said. "The mighty dollar so often wins."

"It's a sad truth."

Sergeant Hall returned. "They are all on their way, sir."

Parker stood, motioned for Samson, and said, "I'll leave now."

As they started to head out the door connecting the colonel's inner office with his outer office, four men came toward Parker. Samson went wild as the third man passed, barking and jumping all over him. He wouldn't even heel for Parker. The man gave Samson a hand signal to lie down, and

Samson instantly hit the ground, like he had in the photo.

Parker looked over at the sergeant, looked back through the connecting door at the colonel still seated at his desk but in a direct line of sight for what just happened and nodded, his face grim. Six men showed up in all. Parker hadn't even had a chance to disappear with Samson yet.

Hall shuffled all six men outside, then returned, shutting the outer door behind him. The colonel then called him into his office. Hall was there for less than a minute, shutting the colonel's office door behind him.

Parker looked over at Hall and asked, "Any other handlers on base?"

"Some with little experience but not the same familiarity Samson would recognize."

"Besides," Sandy said, "wasn't that fairly definitive?"

"It's definitive that Samson knows that third guy well, yes," Parker said in a low voice. "But now we have to place him at the airport."

"If he had anything to do with Ronnie's death, well, his career is over," Hall said.

"And should be a hell of a lot more than that," Sandy snapped. "A man lost his life. I don't know whether Ronnie was part of this nightmare or an innocent victim, but somebody needs to be held accountable for it."

The sergeant gave her a sharp nod, turned and left.

Not sure what to do with themselves and whether they were still supposed to go to their quarters or not, and with Samson still lying comfortably nearby, as he had in the hangar, Parker turned to look at Sandy. "Did you recognize any of the men?"

She shook her head. "Not at first glance."

The colonel called out for them to enter. They stepped

back inside.

Then the colonel had Hall bring in the six suspects.

All six men stood very straight, hands clasped behind their backs, staring ahead.

The colonel rose, joined Parker, leaned in and whispered, "Check out their faces and see if anybody looks familiar."

Parker stepped forward as the colonel did.

The colonel spoke to the men standing at attention. "This is Samson. The dog that went missing. He has obviously been recovered and will be heading stateside at some point today. How many of you have worked with him?"

Two men stepped forward. "And the other four of you, have you had no contact with him?"

The first man spoke up. "I've been out on assignments with him, but I've never worked with him myself."

The colonel nodded. "Dismissed, Private."

He saluted, stepped back, turned and marched out.

The colonel questioned them all, and it was apparent only the two who had stepped forward had handled Samson. The other three were dismissed.

He looked at the remaining two men and asked, "What is your relationship with the dog?"

The first man, identified as Corporal Gregg, replied, "I worked with Samson when he was younger, but then he ended up as Corporal Lewis's, then Corporal Fallon's dog. Corporal Fallon was fairly protective, kept Samson isolated more or less."

The colonel turned to the man beside him. "What about you, Corporal Mergans? You worked with Samson a lot, didn't you?"

"I was the sub for Corporal Fallon, yes," Corporal Mergans replied hesitantly. "We work with a lot of dogs. I have some specialties that I've been working on with all the dogs that come through here."

Parker studied him. His manner was a little stiff, but then he was also standing in front of his colonel being questioned. A good reason to make most people uneasy. Even those with nothing to hide. He looked over and said, "Could you give Samson a few commands as subtly as possible so I would not know you were actually giving them?"

"Corporal Mergans," the colonel ordered.

The man nodded, gave Samson the command to sit. Samson sat. He then gave him a command to come. Samson walked forward to the end of the leash, looked back at Parker. Free from Parker, Samson continued forward and lay down at the man's feet.

The corporal leaned down, gave him a good scratch and smiled down at him. Samson appeared to be comfortable, but it wasn't the same type of happy unfailing obedience he had given the other man.

Colonel Barek looked at Parker.

Parker shrugged, nodded and said, "Thank you. You're dismissed."

Mergans turned and marched out.

Parker turned toward the last man standing. "Corporal Gregg, the same."

"Sure," Corporal Gregg replied, puzzled. "Do I get an explanation why?"

The commander shook his head. "No. You don't. At least not at this stage."

Parker took Samson a few feet away, and he came willingly. But the dog's gaze was on the man across from him. Parker then walked away and stood off to the far side, as he had in the hangar, and, when he turned to look back, Samson once again lay at the man's feet. Not touching but a foot away, just happy.

Parker thought about the photo of Samson comfortably ensconced and nodded to the colonel.

"Corporal Gregg, can you tell me where you were last evening between nineteen and twenty-one hundred hours?" the colonel asked.

Corporal Gregg let a whisper of emotion cross his face and replied, "I was in the barracks, sir."

"Do you have anybody who can vouch for that?"

Corporal Gregg stiffened, his gaze going to Parker, then back to the colonel. He knew he couldn't question why when given a direct command. "I'm not sure. I took a shower and spent some time alone. I was on my laptop, just generally relaxing. I went for a walk after dinner."

"Did you speak with anybody? Did anybody see you?" the colonel asked, writing down notes.

Parker thought about what he just said and how crowded the base was and how impossible it would be to not come in contact with somebody.

"You must have seen somebody?" Parker asked deliberately, trying to keep his tone monotone. "I can't walk ten steps without meeting somebody here."

"Seeing somebody doesn't mean you actually know who they are," Corporal Gregg said. He went to shove his hands in his pockets but realized where he was and pulled them out again. "I'll try to think, sir, but, off the top of my head, nobody comes to mind."

The colonel nodded. "In that case, I'll speak to you in a

couple hours." He thought about it, checked his clock, and said, "Report back here at thirteen hundred hours."

Gregg saluted. "Yes, sir." He took two steps back, turned and marched out.

The colonel waited until Gregg left, asked Hall to wait with Sandy in his outer office and then spoke to Parker. "Well?"

"I would say it was him," Parker said slowly. "But we have to place him there. Fingerprints at the hangar could easily be explained away. It is easy on a base like this to see people, but they become just faces to you after a while."

The colonel looked at him curiously. "How many months did you do over here?"

"Two tours," Parker replied. "I understand that sense of loneliness. But, as far as Corporal Gregg goes, Samson obviously has a relationship of some kind with him from what we witnessed in your outer office and what we saw in the photos."

"All we really see in the photos is a dog lying in front of a bunch of hanging clothing."

"Except for that face," Parker reminded him.

The colonel nodded slowly. "It is hidden enough that it'll be hard to prove."

"Exactly. But he got there somehow, and that means wheels. Would he have to sign them out, or would he happen to have any assigned to him? Do you have any tracking devices on them?"

The colonel gave a half smile. "We do keep track of our people and our vehicles. I'll get the sergeant on it. You have about an hour and a half left until your service. I believe you fly out this afternoon?"

"I think it's six, err, eighteen hundred hours," Parker

replied.

"Eighteen hundred. Right. Although that may have to get pushed back, depending on how our investigation goes."

"Well, I hope it doesn't, sir. Sandy and I have funeral arrangements for our brothers back stateside."

"Sad business, indeed. How is it that you got asked to look after this dog?"

Parker smiled and told him about how Commander Cross had asked Badger to look into a dozen cases. "And this just happened to be one of them."

"It's a damn shame that department has been closed down," the colonel said. "It seems like more and more departments are shutting down than are getting budget money."

"I think that's a constant state of affairs when it comes to government and military spending."

"It is, indeed. I'll see you at the service in an hour and a half." And he returned to the paperwork on his desk.

Obviously dismissed, Parker nodded, called Samson to him, grabbed his rope leash and walked outside. He saw Sandy with Sergeant Hall, waiting. "We're free until the service."

"Was it him do you think?" Sandy asked.

"I think so, yes," Parker said. "We still have to identify the men who kidnapped you."

"I've got a lookout for the man with the big nose," Hall said. "I've asked around, and he does hang out with somebody who possibly matches the tall thin second man. So far, we haven't found them on base though."

"Curious and curiouser," Sandy said in low tones. "Where do we spend the next hour and a half?"

Parker hesitated, looked over at Hall. He looked back at

them, raised an eyebrow but didn't offer anything. Parker finally said, "We can walk around the base together. We can go back to the barracks and stay there until our appointed time, or we can go to the mess and grab yet another coffee."

Sandy winced. "Honestly none of those sound great."

"I know. But we can be private and alone at the barracks." He looked over at Hall. "Providing there is security?"

"I'll make sure there is," he said. "If you wait here for a moment, I'll go check with the colonel." He disappeared inside and came back a few minutes later, his face completely unreadable.

"I never know if that face means good news or bad news," Parker said to him.

The sergeant gave a bark of laughter. "That's why we do it," he said. "It keeps you all guessing."

"It doesn't help us feel any better about the situation," Sandy muttered.

"Maybe not," he said. "But we're the ones who need to get to the bottom of it, not you."

She sighed heavily. "True."

They walked past a washroom, and Sandy said, "I need a pit stop." With a half smile at the men, she headed for the washroom. After she used the facility, she walked up to the sink, washed her hands thoroughly and tried to straighten up the tendrils of hair that were everywhere. She stared in the mirror for a long moment and shook her head. She returned outside. Thankfully the men were still where she'd left them. "I was afraid for a moment that you'd be gone," she confessed.

"Not happening," Parker said with a smile, holding out his hand. "I'll promise to do anything I can to stop you from getting kidnapped again."

"Good," she said, gratefully linking her hand with his. "Once was more than enough."

They continued on to the barracks, and, as they stepped inside, Sandy gasped.

The sergeant looked at her. "What's the matter?"

"Our bags are gone," she said in stunned disbelief. She walked forward, looked around, checked under the beds and turned to look back at him. "Did you have our bags taken somewhere?"

Hall frowned, shook his head and said, "Stay here."

He stepped back out but closed the door hard behind them. She looked over at Parker. "All of my personal things are in there."

"I hear you," he said. "I've still got my wallet, but my personal gear is gone."

"Somebody better not have stolen our stuff," she said, her tone turning dark. "I'll upend this base if that's the case."

"Take it easy," Parker said. "Remember? We're flying out today, so maybe they needed the space for someone else, and we would get moved."

She frowned and thought about it. "Did my stuff go missing when the men took me earlier?"

"That's possible. Wait. We came back here though, didn't we?" He thought about it and shook his head, "No. We went straight to the mess hall tent. So, our bags could have been removed then."

He walked around the area, but there was nothing to see.

He sat down on the side of the bed, called Samson over and let him hop up. He was pretty sure the dog wasn't allowed on the bed, but none of those rules seemed to make any difference anymore. He let the dog stretch out, scrubbing his ears. So far, Samson had been more like a pet than a working dog. "That's the life, isn't it, buddy? You'll end up going home and thinking you found Nirvana."

"Except a lot of these dogs love to work," Sandy said. "They live for it."

"I know. But that's not happening in Samson's case."

"Unless somebody takes him on as a working dog. There's no reason, with his training, that he couldn't work for a fire department or for the police or an airport," she said. "It would make him happy."

"Wow. That's an interesting idea," Parker said, as he looked down at Samson. "I'm the one who doesn't have a way to make a living. I was looking at building houses but ..."

"If you build your house, you could build dog pens and start training these guys."

"I'm not a trainer. I'm not a handler."

"Do you think it's hard to learn?"

Parker shook his head. "I really don't know. What I saw from those six handlers in the colonel's office, it's more than just training the dog. Where Samson here is already trained, it's a case of his handler needing training." He burst out laughing. "It gives me something to think about at least."

"I also think it's a good career choice for both of you," she said. "You're still part of that whole defender-protector mold. Not sure you'll shake that off to go build houses for rich people."

"How about houses for poor people like me?" he asked with a grin. "It's not like any of us coming out of the military have massive bank accounts."

"Isn't that the truth," she said. "It's another reason why I don't want to lose my personal belongings, my purse was with them."

"Right. All your traveling documents and IDs too?"

She nodded. "Along with the picture of my brother," she said. "I brought it to place on his coffin. I didn't want him to be a nameless, faceless box as we fly home."

He stared at her, surprised. "I never even thought to do something like that," he confessed, "but what a great idea."

"Not so great," she said, "if somebody has stolen it."

"Well, let's hope for the best. It can't be far. We're on a base, so it should still be here. We could go back and check where you were being held. Obviously those men knew it was empty."

She hopped to her feet. "Let's go. Maybe they moved our stuff back there, so they'd have a chance to go through it. We can take somebody with us to make sure we don't get into any trouble."

Parker stood, smiled, crossed his hand over his heart and said, "Break my heart. But you're right. I didn't protect you last time."

There was such a hard note in his tone, she reached out and stroked his cheek. "You weren't with me, remember? No guilt. No blame." She leaned in and kissed him gently and said, "Come on. Let's go take a look."

PARKER LED THE way. He kept a decent grip on Samson's leash but had no fear he'd take off. Parker was more afraid somebody would come and jerk the dog from his hand. And he had no reason for wondering that except the dog had already gone missing once, and Parker didn't want Samson to go missing a second time, not on his watch.

Holding an equally tight grip on his arm was Sandy as

she walked at his side. "Are we still being followed?"

"I doubt we'll shake the security as long as we're on the base. It's not worth them getting into trouble over."

She chuckled at that. "I guess in a place like this everybody has a duty, and everybody needs to keep the huge machine rolling."

"Exactly. You know how this works." He nudged her arm toward the buildings ahead. "Do you recognize which one it was?"

Her footsteps slowed as she contemplated the barracks in front of them. "I think it was the last one," she said. "When I came rushing back out, I didn't see much, just more barracks."

He nodded. "We should do a quick search of them all."

With her still gripping his arm, he opened the door, stepped into the first one, did a quick check and stepped out. They went through the next three.

At the fifth one, Parker stepped in, Sandy at his side. She noticed something sticking out from under a cot, and she bent down. She pulled out her purse. Her cry of delight warmed his heart.

She pulled out her passport, then wallet. Checked inside. "Everything is still here, even the picture of my brother and all my cash," she said with a big smile. She slung her purse strap over her head to rest against her body.

"What about the rest of our bags?" He crouched, twisted his head down and looked under the cots. "No sign of them."

"Let's keep looking," she said. "If we never get anything else back, I'm totally okay with this."

He understood how she felt. These were his sentiments exactly. The picture of her brother, her passport, IDs, wallet, all of that was much more important. She clutched the purse to the front of her body. "Good," he said. "Hang on to that."

She gave him the briefest of smiles. "Don't worry. I intend to. I'm hanging on to you, and I'm hanging on to my purse." Then she laughed. "And you're hanging on to me, and you're hanging on to Samson. We are quite the trio."

"And let's hope that we are completely overreacting," he murmured. As they stood outside the building where they found her purse, he looked around. "What do you want to do now?"

"More empty barracks are here. What do you think?"

He nodded. "As long as they're empty, we can do a quick check."

They proceeded to check nine more empty barracks, and, when they came to one that actually had a voice on the other side, at Parker's knock, the voice stopped.

Parker said, "We're looking for two missing bags. Any sign of them in there?"

A tousled head popped out, looking like he had just woken up. "I don't know, man. Let me check." He came back out a few moments later with two bags. "Are these yours?" He looked back inside. "You guys supposed to be here?"

Sandy gave a cry of joy, reaching for her bag, and slung it over her back.

Parker reached for his own. Still holding Samson's leash, they were forced to separate slightly. Parker looked at the guy and grinned. "No. We got moved up to the front, but our bags didn't come with us."

The guy just rolled his eyes and said, "Figures. If you don't mind, I'm heading back to bed now." The door slammed in their face.

But they had what they needed, and they were happy. So, with no more wasted time, Parker grabbed Sandy's hand and marched a steady pace to where the ceremony would be, Samson happy to join them.

"Right. We're almost out of time, aren't we?" she asked, walking faster to keep up.

"Sorry," he said. "I don't mean to make you run."

"We don't have time for niceties," she stated and started to gain speed on him.

He gave her a crooked grin, picked up speed, and within minutes they were almost where the ceremony would take place.

Slightly out of breath, they arrived a hair early to stand, bags at their feet, breathing hard, as they were confronted with the sight of six coffins.

Parker heard Sandy catch her breath. Almost like a physical blow to both of them.

He gripped her fingers hard. "Stand steady," he whispered.

Maybe that was what she needed to hear. Maybe he needed to hear that himself. He watched her back stiffen, and her shoulders straighten. She gave a hard nod. "It's what he would want too."

Parker stared at the names on the tops of the coffins. Hating to see his brother like this. Hating this end for him. To know she was going through the exact same emotions helped but also hurt. He'd have done anything to have saved people from this. Other men and women stood at the other coffins. Other family members.

He could almost hear his brother's voice in the back of his head, whispering against his ear, *Who'd have thought we'd get to this point, bro?*

He smiled, forcing back the emotions. Down the road, when Parker was away from the immediacy of it all, he'd take time to grieve, time to remember his brother for who he was.

He could feel fingers gripping his and realized, for all her attempts to be strong, tears slowly rolled down Sandy's cheeks. That made it that much harder to keep his own back.

She gripped his hand and walked forward to the second coffin where she dropped his hand and placed hers on top of the coffin and bowed her head for a long moment. He placed his on the same coffin beside hers. This had been Parker's brother's best friend. He deserved as good a send-off as anybody could give him. Silently Parker and Sandy stood shoulder to shoulder, and then he shifted to his brother's coffin and held out his left hand so he had one hand on each.

She followed suit until they were both standing in the circle of his arms, each with a hand on the two coffins. It was one of the most emotional and momentous moments of his life.

Trying to say goodbye to his brother and yet not ready to let go. He wanted to be strong for his brother. In the background he could almost hear his brother saying, *You're trying too hard, bro. Let it go.*

Parker sniffled slightly. Sandy turned in his arms, reached up and kissed him on the cheek. He tightened his arms around her and cuddled her close. When they could, they both stepped back, an arm still wrapped around each other, and they stood tall.

The ceremony itself was quick, emotional and incredibly powerful. When they were done, he watched as the crowd slightly dispersed. But he had absolutely no inclination to move. Neither did Sandy. She stayed with her head tucked against his chest.

Samson lay at their feet. He'd been at attention up until everybody started to disperse, and then he relaxed.

Parker resolved to do some training, so he was up to speed with a dog like Samson. He was extremely well-trained. And it shouldn't take too much for Samson to learn to work with Parker too. Maybe he could talk to somebody back home about that. It would be a good investment in both him and Samson. Potentially they should be contracting their skills out. Or rather, Samson's skills out.

Parker squeezed Sandy gently and whispered, "Are you ready to leave?"

She reached up, brushed away the tears and smiled gently. "There won't be much point in staying," she whispered.

As they turned to look, only family members remained. It looked like they didn't want to leave either. "Do you want to talk to them?"

Sandy nodded. "Sure," she said and slipped out of his arms, walked over, spoke quietly to the other grieving family members, hugged them and returned to Parker. She smiled up at him. "We don't leave for another four hours, right?"

"They moved our flights earlier, I thought ..." He checked his watch. "We leave at five o'clock."

"Good. The sooner, the better." She walked over to her brother's coffin, placed the image on top, secured by the double-stick tape on the back, and kissed the wood, then pressed her hand to it gently. "Bye, Jeremy," she whispered hoarsely. She walked back over and looped her arm with Parker's. He leaned in and softly kissed her forehead.

"They will load the coffins in the trucks. We can grab something to eat, since we missed lunch, then head to the airport."

"My stomach is in knots, but I go where you go."

They watched as the coffins with their brothers' bodies inside were loaded into trucks. It was a somber moment. It still didn't feel final because they hadn't had their funerals in the States yet. Parker and Sandy clung to each other, and Samson seemed to just know it was a moment to be quiet. He stood tall, whining slightly. Parker pet the dog on the top of his head. "Good boy," he said.

"It's hard to leave them," Sandy said, "but it's time."

Sergeant Hall came up behind them. "You found your bags," he said, surprise in his voice. "Where were they?"

Parker explained how they found them, and Sergeant Hall frowned. "More bad news," he said. He shook his head. "We do have more men in the colonel's office. So, if you've got a moment, we should go over and take a look. Maybe you will recognize one of them from being here at the base."

"Lead the way, Sergeant Hall."

He nodded solemnly. "Of course."

They fell into step behind him, now holding hands, Samson eager to be moving forward and quite comfortable in the circumstances. The sergeant looked down at Samson and said, "He appears to be behaving himself."

"Considering we were instructed to keep him in the cage at all times, he's been incredibly easy to work with."

"Most of the K9s are extremely well-trained," Sergeant Hall said. "It's hard to go wrong having a dog like him at home."

"I have to talk to Commander Cross when I get stateside," Parker said.

"Right." Hall shook his head. "It's too bad that division shut down. I understand why but ..." His voice trailed off. He motioned up ahead. "We're just down around this corner."

They followed him to the colonel's familiar office and stepped inside. The colonel greeted them and pointed at a corner. "Feel free to drop your gear there."

Parker placed his stuff down, then grabbed Sandy's to-go bag and stacked it on top. He knew she had no intention of leaving her purse anywhere but strapped around her body.

Colonel Barek said, "Take a seat beside me." Two chairs were to the side of his desk. He motioned at Sergeant Hall. "Let's begin."

The sergeant disappeared through the open door.

The colonel said, "We will bring in each soldier. They will identify themselves. They will make a turn so you can take a look at their profile, and then they will step out. At any point, if you want to see somebody longer or again, just let me know."

He could feel Sandy's startle of surprise. But Parker knew this needed to happen. He wrapped his hand with hers, holding on tight, giving her support through his grip. She did not have to be afraid. He was staying.

The first corporal came through the door, stopped in front of them. "Corporal Jarvis, sir." He turned ninety degrees, then walked out. This happened for each man.

Parker looked at her, and she shook her head. The colonel looked at her and asked, "Anybody?"

"Not yet," she said. But, as soon as the next man stepped in, she stiffened. And a strangled squeak escaped.

"Corporal Rodgers, sir." He turned a full circle and started to walk away.

The colonel looked at her. "We will have him sit off to one side."

She nodded, but her fingers were gripping Parker so

hard that she was leaving indents from her nails. The next one came in and then two more. She shook her head after each one left.

Sergeant Hall stepped back in. "We have one more," he said. He pulled open the door and let the last man in.

He spoke his name. "Corporal Daley, sir." He turned and walked away.

Sandy nodded her head as soon as he turned away.

Sergeant Hall stopped him at the doorway and signaled for the other corporal to return.

Parker faced her. "Are you okay?"

She let out a slow exhale and turned to look at him and the colonel. "Yes, I'm fine. Those are the two men who kidnapped me."

CHAPTER 8

THE COLONEL LOOKED at her, his voice hard, his gaze even harder. "Are you certain?"

She studied the two men, both of them staring straight ahead, but she could see the muscles twitching in their jaws.

She nodded emphatically. "Yes," she said. "They are the men who kidnapped me, who took me to another building and who gave me the third degree about Parker and why we were here. When they suspected they were about to be caught, they dragged me from the first building, smacked me hard on my cheek"—she turned to show the colonel the bruise on her slightly puffy face—"then they dragged me to another barracks."

The colonel stood, walked around to stand in front of the two men. "Soldiers. What do you two have to say for yourselves?"

The men looked at him but didn't say a word. Silence ensued for a long moment, and the colonel finally nodded and said, "Fine. Don't speak. You will eventually." He turned to face the door and called out to Sergeant Hall.

The sergeant stepped back in. "Take them to the brig," he said. "I want to know who is in their circles and what business they have to do with the theft going on in this base. And what was their role in Ronnie's death."

As the corporals left with the sergeant, Corporal Daley

turned back and said, "Sir. I had nothing to do with his death."

With a hand motion at his sergeant, the colonel had both men separated. He brought Corporal Daley back in. "Explain, Corporal?"

"I am part of a team stealing supplies from this base," he said painfully. "But I had nothing to do with Ronnie's death."

"Who did?" the colonel demanded.

The man shrugged. After that, the colonel didn't show any mercy. He fired question after question at the corporal.

When he was done, Parker asked a few of his own.

Sandy had nothing to say; she just watched as this soldier was pummeled with questions. She had her phone in her hand and was videotaping it. Not to have for later but to make sure she understood what was going on.

At one point, the corporal seemed to falter. The colonel pounced. "I want names. I want dates. I want details," he ordered.

The sergeant returned with a notepad, pen and a tape recorder. He sat Daley down and said, "From the beginning, Corporal."

The corporal, by now, realizing just how extremely serious his state was, said, "I'm willing to help on everything. But I did not have anything to do with Ronnie's murder."

"If it is connected, Corporal, it won't make a damn bit of difference. Because, once you are in, you are in. You don't get to pick and choose which part the gang does that you do not partake in. You don't get to say I am part of the making money but not part of the taking the responsibility for the gang. It does not work that way," the colonel said and glared at him.

He got up and walked over to Sergeant Hall and discussed something quietly off to the side. The sergeant walked over and stood in front of Parker and Sandy. "Let's take you two to the mess tent. We have more business to conduct here."

Parker stood, and Sandy did too but slower. She hooked her arm through his and let the sergeant lead them in another maze back to the mess hall. It was already three-thirty p.m. "Wow. Time is flying."

"It is, indeed. We have to get to the airport soon."

"We need to get some more food for Samson."

"Shit," Parker said. He sat down and pulled Samson over and gave him a rub on his face. "I'm not used to looking after a dog. It'll take me a bit to get used to. Sorry, bud. Maybe if the sergeant comes with us, we'll get something from the supply clerk."

The sergeant nodded. "I can even get paperwork if need be. We can't have the dog starving, now that he's back safe."

"Exactly," Sandy replied.

"We should grab a few bottles of water for him too," Parker said.

The sergeant grabbed several bottles of water, a plastic dish and brought it all back. He opened up one of the bottles, filled the dish and put it down in front of Samson.

Samson emptied it in no time.

"Now let's get him some dry kibble."

"A few sample bags would be great," Parker said.

"We'll stop at supply on our way," the sergeant said.

That was the first inkling that Hall wouldn't be cutting loose from them at any point. Sandy smiled up at him. "Sorry that you're on babysitting duty."

Hall chuckled. "I'm okay. Gets me out of a lot of paperwork."

Parker laughed. "I won't miss that."

"I understand you are leaving the service?"

Parker nodded. "I wasn't really thinking about it before, but my brother's death cinched it for me."

"I understand," the sergeant said. "We find deaths like that either send you one way or the other. But rarely do you ever waffle in the middle."

"With good reason," Parker said. "Jerry gave his life to the military. I'm not sure I want to end up in the same place. I loved it here. I loved my years here, but I think it's time to move on. There's just me and my dad now. I would hate to die in combat and have a stranger arriving at my father's door to let him know his other son is now gone."

"Good point," the sergeant said. "The military's been my life, but I'm one of four boys. So my family would be fine."

"I'm glad you have a big family, but even the loss of one member is never good," Sandy said, smiling up at him. "Make sure you stay safe. Life is short, and the loss of my brother has shown me that I still want to do a lot of things, and it's not all tied to the military."

"That is the one thing about it," the sergeant said. "It's all encompassing. It's a completely different world. The rules are different. The punishments are different, but the one thing that you do have to do is follow the rules or else."

"As we've come to see," she said. "What will happen to those young corporals?"

His face turned grim. "Nothing good," he said. "They threw their lives away, and not just because of the theft but being involved in the murder of a fellow serviceman ..." He shook his head. "Well, you can just imagine."

"Those men couldn't have been more than twenty-five years old," she protested.

"They may not have been," Parker said at her side, "but they were certainly old enough to know right from wrong. Yes, there is a lot of peer pressure, and, yes, they might have gotten in with the wrong crowd, but that's no excuse ..."

"I understand," she said, but her heart was heavy. "It's just hard when you are taking home two servicemen in boxes, as we are. Seeing the coffins all lined up, you realize what these men are here for. It's just a shame Rodgers and Daley started out like our brothers and yet are now involved in this mess."

"They also likely benefited quite a bit from it too," the sergeant said. "Keep that in mind. Unfortunately it doesn't seem to matter how big a machine, and maybe because this machine is too big, but there will always be corruption to be corralled, and liars and cheaters have to be dealt with. But to murder one of your own countrymen, who's over here in service of our country, that'll never go down well," he said.

Parker and Sandy nodded solemnly. Hall was right, but it still did not make the situation any less sad. "Okay. I'll head over to the supply and see if I can get you some dog food, and then I will escort you to the airport."

"Much appreciated," Parker said.

The sergeant nodded and stood. "Don't leave from this spot."

They watched as he headed to the door, spoke to two men, and he pointed them out.

"Wow. Was that a babysitting duty hand off to those two?" she asked.

"Yes, it was, at least for a few minutes. I'd expect him to take us to the airport but plans change. And I might have heard wrong," Parker said. "It doesn't matter because we're going home."

She gave him a sad smile. "Yeah, we are. And thank heavens for that. I don't think I could stick around much longer."

"It'll still be tough for a while, even when we get stateside."

"I know. Jeremy will be cremated. And we'll have a celebration of life for him at the family home."

"My father wants to bury Jerry in the family plot."

"Sounds perfect," she said. "Everybody gets to deal with grief in their own way. I just don't think I'll deal with it quickly."

"No," Parker said. "I'm not sure we'll ever deal with it. I think I'll always turn around and expect to see Jerry walking in the door. Even now I keep hearing his voice in my head, telling me to lighten up."

"Oh, that's so Jerry and so Jeremy. I really loved the fact that they enjoyed life. They lived it to the max, and they died doing what they loved."

HALL—HAVING REJOINED THEM, carrying a few more packets of food samples for Samson, plus bottled water for them all—then had them in the vehicle to transport them to their flight. Arriving at the airport, Parker held the door open so Samson could hop from the vehicle. He grabbed his duffel bag and Sandy's backpack and waited until she got out of the vehicle on the other side with her purse.

They thanked Sergeant Hall for the escort and walked around to the back of the vehicle. The sergeant headed into the hangar to talk to somebody.

Parker smiled at Sandy. "Well, we made it. Didn't think we'd ever get here."

"I know," she said with a half smile. "We certainly have plenty of food for Samson now."

"It's a long trip."

"I suspect Samson will sleep most of the way."

"He'll have to be crated, but I need a place to put this stuff down and to get his crate out."

"Let's take our stuff over to the side of the building. And then we can come back and get the crate."

They walked everything over to the shady side of the building, dropped it all and together walked back to the vehicle and picked up the crate. With the crate once again with their bags, Sandy said, "Not exactly an international airport, is it?"

"No," Parker said. "It sure isn't. But it's one of the smaller ones we have here. So, a whole lot less amenities than even some of the others."

She nodded. "That's what I thought. I've been in a couple military airports, but they were much bigger than this."

"Right, I have too," he said. "Feel free to sit on my duffel bag, if you want."

"No," she said. "I'm happy to walk around for a bit. I kind of want to go into the building, but, at the same time, I don't."

He understood perfectly. "Not sure that we'd even be allowed in actually. After the last time," he said with a broken laugh. "Not that that had anything to do with us but ..."

She stretched her arms overhead and did several long-limbed stretches that showed off her form perfectly.

But he knew she was completely unconscious of what she was doing. She was just taking some of the kinks out of her spine. "You should be able to sleep better tomorrow."

"I know, but, in the meantime, we'll pretzel our way through a long flight."

He nodded. "Yes, but this is the last one. And there's something so final, almost reassuring about that."

"I know, but, after everything that's happened already, it feels like we'll never get there. It feels like the last leg, but this leg is a huge hurdle. It shouldn't feel like that, but it does."

"That's because of what we have been through," he said. "I, for one, will feel better when we take off."

"I won't," she joked. "Not until we land safely."

"Do we need to say anything to the sergeant before he leaves?" Parker asked, as he stood in front of his gear, watching the sergeant talking with two other men.

Then the sergeant looked at him, lifted a hand in a wave and hopped into the vehicle. Even as they watched, he drove off, leaving a plume of dust behind. "I'll say no then," Sandy said in a comical voice. "I guess we're not friends after all."

At that, Parker joked, "No, we're just two wild cards in the night."

"They should have lounge chairs here. How long do we have to wait?"

"I'm not sure. The flight's not just us going home. The coffins have to be brought in as well. The other family members aren't active servicemen, and they are likely flying commercial."

At that, she fell silent. "Right. Maybe that's why we can't go in. Maybe the coffins are already here."

"I don't know. A large plane is on the tarmac, and it had

all the doors open and the big loading bay dropped in the back. It's also possible the coffins have already been loaded."

Her voice caught in the back of her throat as if she tried to speak but couldn't. Finally she said, "I just want to go home." This time her voice was small, almost choking on grief.

In concern, Parker held out his arms, and she walked into them. She burrowed in deep and just hung on. He could feel her shoulders shaking and knew she was ready to break at any time.

As trips went, this had already been a rough one. But the things that had happened since they'd been here ... He was surprised she'd still held it all together as it was. She'd been brave and courageous, and he admired that, and he also appreciated it was easier than having a woman in tears all the time.

"There are likely chairs inside. You want me to go look?"

She shook her head. "No, we shouldn't have to wait that long." She settled down on the dirt, leaning back against the hangar. "I hate that we're back here though."

"There shouldn't be any dead bodies inside this time," he joked.

She smiled. "There better not be." She glanced around and said, "We never did hear how any of this worked out, did we?"

"No, no, we didn't. We found those two men, but we don't know who else might have been involved."

As they watched, another vehicle came and parked up in the front. One man got out and went into the hangar. They watched quietly but nothing else happened. "Where's the staff?" she asked.

"You mean, the pilot? Might not even be here yet."

"Right," she said. "Not an international airline of course," she half joked. "Maybe that was him who just arrived."

But the guy stepped out of the hangar, walked back to his car, started it and drove off again.

"I hope that wasn't our pilot," Parker said. They waited longer and then heard an odd popping sound inside the hangar.

Sandy didn't appear to notice but maybe, from where he'd been standing, it sounded a little more like something he didn't want to recognize. But Samson, with a growl in the back of his throat, had him going.

He jerked Sandy to her feet and ordered, "Stay behind me."

"Why? What happened?" she cried out, stumbling over the bags they had on the ground.

"I just heard an odd popping sound, and Samson's upset too."

"I didn't hear a sound."

"I did," he said and tugged her back toward the rear of the building. "People know we're standing here. Which means, if they want to shoot us, we're sitting ducks."

She picked up the pace and raced beside him. "And we've got no place to go, and we've got no wheels," she cried out. "Please be wrong."

In the back was another big door. Parker peered in through one of the windows but couldn't see anything. "It's damn hard to see anything through here," he complained. "I want to go inside and take a look."

But Sandy pulled on his arm. "No," she ordered. "If you heard gunshots, that means somebody in there is armed and doesn't mind pulling the trigger. We're not walking into that."

"If we don't walk into it, the shooter will walk out with it."

She stared up at him. "The only thing we can do is go cross-country."

"And that won't work out so well for us because there's no real area to hide here."

"But there is a ditch," she said, pointing.

He looked at it and frowned.

"You know what? It's our only option. The ditch or we go inside or try to get to the plane," she said.

"If it's only the ditch or inside the plane, then it won't be hard for them to find us."

Just then they heard a door slam on the other side. Sandy grabbed his hand and said, "Come on."

The two raced to the back by the fence where a ditch ran down in a slight shallow.

With the three of them flat, Parker held Samson close, wondering just how bad this would get.

There was a shout out, "Hey, where are you two?"

Parker kept Samson silent with a hand over his muzzle.

"Where the hell have they gone now?" the voice said.

It was a voice he didn't recognize. And that didn't help much either. He had his phone in his hand, sending messages via Badger again. But Parker couldn't do much except lie here and wait. When he heard the crunch of footsteps coming toward them, he swore softly. He looked at Sandy. She gazed back at him, fear in her eyes.

He realized it would be up to him and Samson, but they did have the element of surprise.

With that goal in mind, he let go of Samson's leash. Just as the dog was about to rush up over the ditch, he heard the stranger say, "There you are."

Parker snapped out, "Samson, attack."

With a growl coming from the back of his throat, Samson went after the gunman, who even now held a rifle, pointing toward Sandy.

Parker bolted from the ditch as the rifle turned to face him as the newest threat. But Samson lunged and snagged the man's forearm, his weight pulling the man down as the rifle fired. Gravel split upward at Parker's feet. But he was already on the gunman. The rifle dropped, and the man screamed as Parker pounded him into the ground—his fist hitting him in the face again and again.

Through the din he heard Sandy call out, "Stop. Stop."

Finally Parker sank his knees on the man's chest to see the gunman was unconscious. Even Samson lay at his side, staring up at Parker, his jaw locked on the gunman's wrist. Samson was looking for a command to let go.

Parker reached over and said, "Good boy, Samson. Let go." And the dog hesitantly dropped the man's arm and then stood up.

Parker gave Samson a good scratch on his head and showed him lots of admiration.

Sandy had no such restraint. She bent down, wrapped her arms around Samson and held him close. "Jesus," she said. "I don't know what we would have done without him. That rifle was aimed at me."

"I know," Parker said. "And then it was turned on me when he saw me coming. But now we have to go back into that hangar and figure out what happened."

She shook her head. "You know he probably isn't alone."

"Doesn't matter if he is or not," Parker said. He picked

up the weapon. "At least we're not unarmed anymore."

"We can't just leave him here."

He nodded and quickly unlaced the man's boots. With those laces, he tied up his captive's hands and his feet and then rolled him into the ditch. His face was up so, even if the ditch filled with water, he would be okay for a bit. "Come on. Let's go," he said.

She hesitated.

"Inside with me?" he asked. "Or stay behind?"

"Well, in that case, no contest." And she put her hand in his and together, with Samson, they crept up to the hangar.

He looked down at their hands and said, "We stick together."

CHAPTER 9

SANDY HATED THE idea of going back inside, but staying behind and waiting with the injured gunman wasn't ideal either. She wouldn't send Parker into a war if she wasn't there to help out—although not sure what she could do to help as it seemed that Samson and Parker both had this down. Still, she wanted to be where they were.

Gripping his fingers firmly, Sandy followed Parker and Samson as they slipped back to the corner of the hangar. Parker peered in through the back window again and shook his head. "I don't see anything."

"Not good," she said. Her voice was a low whisper, trying to stop it from carrying in the dead afternoon. "There should be more people here. We're leaving, for crying out loud. There should be coffins of servicemen."

"But we're early, remember?"

"Was that deliberate?" she asked softly.

He glanced at her. "I hope not because that could mean Sergeant Hall was involved."

She nodded. "I know. That just occurred to me."

They went around to the far side of the hangar and came up toward the plane side. The building was solid, secure and who knew what was going on inside. "The best scenario would be if there is just the one man, and we've already taken him out. But I did hear shots earlier, and I'm afraid somebody might be bleeding out inside."

"In that case let's go check. I might be able to save him still."

He opened the door to the office and pushed it wide. Nothing was there. No one waited for them.

Sandy couldn't see anyone. Following along with Samson at full alert leading the way, they pushed opened the door into the hangar. And they stayed crouched down low, in case shots were fired. But there was nothing.

From her position she could see a foot. "Let me go," she whispered.

He nodded and said, "First we check out the hangar to make sure you won't get hurt."

She chafed at that. But it made sense. Didn't matter what the medical emergency was, you always made sure it was safe to enter no matter what. She stood up with him, and they slowly entered.

As she went past a section, she saw a hammer. She reached out and snagged it.

He looked at her and the hammer and then gave a nod. "Good girl."

It was foolish, but she felt better having a weapon. It wouldn't do anything against a gun or a knife, but she could create damage with it. And that was one of the things she planned on doing if it got that bad.

As they walked by an area, she could see a man lying on the ground, but the pool of blood around him said he was already too far gone for her to help. She swore softly. His eyes were open and sightless, staring up at the ceiling.

Parker already noticed and tugged her forward. They did a final large sweep around the building, but nobody else appeared to be here.

"Do you think it's just him?"

He shrugged, stopped and slowly circled back around. As they approached the body, another shot was fired and landed in the wood right in front of Parker's head.

They hit the ground. He looked at her, and she said, "I guess not."

He nudged her forward and whispered, "Go into the office."

She quickly shifted around behind him and crept into the office area.

He followed, rifle at the ready, with Samson at his side. Samson was growling deep in his throat.

SANDY CROUCHED IN the office, looking into the main hangar. Suddenly Sandy felt a weapon on the back of her neck. She gasped hard.

Parker turned, looked at her and froze.

All she could see was Parker's face.

He looked at whomever was holding the weapon to her and said, "Leave her out of this."

"Can't do that," the voice said. "She's in the middle of it."

"Two of your men are already in the brig," Parker said. "Two are now dead. What's the point of shooting us?"

"Satisfaction? Who knows? But, with you guys gone, this stays here."

"You heard the sergeant and the colonel today," Parker said.

When she heard that, she realized it wasn't Sergeant Hall standing over her, pushing a gun into her neck. For some reason that made her feel a hell of a lot better. She'd really liked him, and, at least if they had somebody on their side, they had a chance of getting out of this.

"Doesn't matter. If we're going down, we're taking out everyone with us."

"So you'll make sure that, instead of six coffins flying out today, there'll be a dozen?" Parker scoffed at that.

The butt of the gun pressed farther into her neck, making her wince and twist her head.

"Fine," Parker said. "Be that way. But you could get out of this still, you know?"

"There's no getting out of this," the voice said harshly. "Ronnie wasn't supposed to be found so fast. We needed time to deal with his body. It would have been fine but for you two."

"Is that why you hid among the coveralls over there?" Sandy asked suddenly.

There was silence first and then an intake of a hard breath. "You figured that out, did you?"

"Yes," she said. "From the photos. And, of course, Samson."

"Damn dog. I trained him for so many hours, but that training itself is a giveaway."

"Not to mention the fact that Ronnie worked with two men here who happened to be friends of yours."

"On a base like this, everybody is friends, and nobody is friends." The gunman sneered. "They were part of the team. Only Ronnie was giving us trouble."

"Meaning, he wasn't a full-fledged member?"

"Meaning, we were trying to bring him in on it, but he wasn't interested."

"And how did the dog play into this?"

"He didn't. Ronnie opened the cage to give the dog an option to go or to stay. We were trying to move a bunch of gear into our private little stash. We needed the window, and then, when Ronnie let the dog go, all hell broke loose. We weren't sure if he'd done it on purpose, not until we talked to him. That's when we knew he wasn't interested in being a part of it. He didn't know how to get himself out though."

"You took care of him though, didn't you?" Sandy said sadly. "He didn't need to die for that."

"Everybody dies," snapped Corporal Gregg from behind her.

"And who else is in here?" Parker asked.

"If you don't know, ain't no point in me trying to tell you."

"It's the other guy with Ronnie that night," Sandy said. "I didn't recognize him until he was lying in the ditch face up. It took me a while, but he'd been one of the two men who were there that night."

Just then they heard footsteps. "Everything under control?"

"Yeah, sure, Mike. Everything is, except for your buddy," Corporal Gregg said. "He's out of commission. Compliments of these two."

"God damn it, I told Drake to not go on his own like that."

"He's a bit of a cowboy," Gregg said. "You better go get him."

"Ha! He can fucking stay out there in the ditch for a while."

"Oh, how'd you know he's in the ditch?" Gregg asked.

"Watched these guys come back," he said. "Figured out what happened."

"Why didn't you shoot them then?" Gregg asked in exasperation. "Jesus Christ, that would have been the easiest."

"Because they were coming inside. It would make less noise if we kill them inside. You know the shots ring out forever with a hell of an echo in these hills."

"You should go and pop your buddy," Gregg said. "He fucked up big-time."

"I'll talk to him about it," Mike said. "Let me go get him."

But as he turned away, Corporal Gregg lifted his gun and fired.

The new arrival, Mike, dropped to his knees, then fell to his side, a look of complete astonishment on his face.

Sandy cried out, her hand clapping over her mouth. She stared at Parker in shock because, if nothing else, she now knew there was no escape from this. Gregg would take them all out if given a chance.

She watched Samson, who was now on his belly creeping forward, no longer held back by a leash. And she realized all Samson needed was an opening, and Sandy herself was in the way. She was literally blocking the space between Samson and the handler behind her. Would Corporal Gregg be able to control Samson right now because it was his dog? Because Gregg had had a longer relationship with the dog? Yet Samson stared at Gregg like he would take him out no matter what.

How did that work? Where did this dog's loyalties lie?

She stared at Parker, half motioning toward Samson. Parker nodded and held out three fingers for her to count.

She stared at them, her gaze going from his fingers to his eyes. Fear choked her. She could only hope that Gregg was distracted right now.

"Goddamn assholes," Corporal Gregg said. "They never do anything right."

"You have to shoot the guy in the ditch yourself now, don't you?" Parker asked.

"Yeah, and now I'll have a lot of bodies to get rid of," he said in disgust. "Why can't people just take orders? Just follow through and stop questioning things. The military should be good for that, but instead you get all these yahoos who think they know how to do this better. No way they should have been running this, and they sure as hell shouldn't have shot Ronnie here. They should have taken him out to the woods and popped him and left him for the buzzards. Instead they killed him here, thinking enough people would be around that they wouldn't get blamed. What idiots."

Corporal Gregg grabbed Sandy by the shoulder and said, "I want you to stand up slowly."

She said, "I will. Just please don't shoot."

She stood, but now she was an even bigger block between Samson and his handler.

Gregg said, "Now take a few steps forward."

She took one step forward. The doorway was right there.

"Now I want you to go about three more steps."

Her gaze locked on Parker, and she could see the tense lines around his mouth. She realized three more steps would be her death.

Parker held up his fingers—three, two, one. At one, she threw herself out of the office door and to the side. Parker whispered, "Attack." And Samson let loose.

Shots were fired, but she could still hear Samson growling and the man screaming, trying to order Samson to stop.

From where she was, she couldn't figure out who was

who, but Parker was no longer where he'd been, and nothing but chaos was happening in the small space of the office.

Not enough room to fight. Not enough room for Samson to get at anybody. But, as long as that gun was out of commission, then her team had a fighting chance.

Then she saw it. A handgun was just around the corner of the doorway. She raced forward and snatched it. Only she didn't dare shoot, not with men and dog fur flying, fists pounding and men grunting. She fired a shot over their heads. It slowed them, but it didn't stop them.

"Stop, or I'll shoot," she ordered.

Parker pulled back and gave an extremely strong fast uppercut to Gregg's jaw. His head snapped back, and he sank to his knees and went down.

As soon as he went down, Samson went down, his jaw still attached to Gregg's shoulder.

Parker looked at her, his hand reaching around to grab her wrist and to gently remove the handgun from her. "It's over," he whispered.

She stared up at him, wordless.

He pulled her close and repeated, "It's over."

"I sure as hell hope so. We have to get Samson off him."

Parker turned, faced Samson and said, "Samson, stand down."

Samson unhooked his jaw, looked up, whined and lay down in front of his handler.

Corporal Gregg groaned once, shifted, as if trying to get up, and then fell back down again unconscious.

"This is just great," she said. "How does this shit just never quit?"

"It'll stop now," Parker said. "Don't you worry."

She shook her head. "Not only will it not stop but there

will now be a full investigation. They'll push our flight back."

"Maybe," he said. "I don't know. Let's see what happens." Just then his phone rang.

She took a few steps away, crouched to cuddle Samson, who stared at the man who'd spent so much time with the dog. "I'm sorry, Samson," she said. "It really sucks. It really does. And maybe it's the best thing that you're away from here. Because this just adds to your stress again." She gently talked to Samson, calmed him down. She heard part of the conversation behind her.

Parker hung up the phone. She looked up at him. Samson was now half on her lap and half off, the unconscious man still out cold in front of them. "What was that about?"

"That was the colonel, not Commander Cross this time. He was following up on Badger's text I sent earlier. He wanted to know more details. I gave him an update on what happened here. He's sending out a sergeant and several more men. He says he's coming himself too."

Sandy frowned. "Great," she said. "More brass. More headache. More paperwork."

He smiled and said, "Sure, but we aren't dead. We don't have bullets in us. We're not recovering from major wounds. So, no matter what they throw at us, remember we can handle it. It's got to be over now."

She shook her head. "I wouldn't count on it. There's just been way too much of this so far. People will go to any lengths to stop themselves from going to jail."

"Not only that," Parker said, "we've got one in the ditch to retrieve."

LEAVING SANDY BESIDE the trussed-up handler and Samson on guard, Parker snuck out of the building and, not seeing anything suspicious, crept along the yard till he got to the ditch. They now had one man down here and one man inside, but he wanted them both together, so he didn't have to worry about both. Keeping an eye out, he dashed into the ditch and froze. He was gone. The man they'd tied up was gone.

He pulled out his phone as he flat-out ran back to the hangar. Sandy's phone kept ringing and ringing in his ear. He hadn't been gone that long, but, God damn it, he'd been gone long enough. He blasted into the hangar, not even giving a shit about being quiet and came to a dead stop.

She stared up at him. But, once again, terror was in her gaze. He spun around to see the man he had left tied up holding a gun pointed at him, his shoulder bloody but his grin ... feral.

Parker looked at Sandy to see she no longer had the weapon he'd left her. He closed his eyes for a long moment and started to swear. "Drake, by any chance?"

Drake laughed. "You should be swearing. You left her with a gun. That wasn't hard to take away from her."

"How did you get out of your ties?" Parker said. "I left you knocked out and tied up."

"You did," Drake said. "I had a knife in my boot, and you didn't check for that. Not that it's very big. It's more of a razor blade and easily missed," he said cheerfully. "Which is exactly why I use it." He motioned the gun at Parker. "Head over there toward her."

Slowly Parker dragged his feet as he considered the possibilities. Once again they were caught up behind a weapon with no actual way out. As he took a few more steps, Drake's eyes shifted. And Parker realized that, pretty soon, he would be facing two of them. As he walked past Corporal Gregg, who was just waking up, Parker kicked him hard on the head to make sure he stayed down.

"Hey, what was that for?" Drake roared. He went to his buddy and dragged him back and away from them.

"I just wanted to make sure he didn't wake up," Parker said. "Of course maybe I should have let him. Because Gregg was intending on killing you too. You know that, right?"

"Doesn't matter," he said. "By the time I've taken care of the three of you, it'll look like you shot everybody anyway."

Parker groaned. And then he realized one thing was missing. Casually he looked around, but he saw no sign of Samson. He reached out a hand; Sandy grabbed it. He squeezed her fingers and sent her a flashing question in his eyes. But she didn't seem to understand.

"Both of you turn and look at me," the gunman snapped. "And, if you're right, then maybe I'll set the scene a little bit better. I just have to think about it."

"If I'm right about what?"

Drake motioned to the man on the floor in front of him. "If Gregg was actually planning on killing me, I need to put things in motion so everything looks like it was him. The two of you got into an altercation, where he shot you guys, and you overcame him, but you still died, and so did he from his wounds."

Parker thought about that.

"I just have to place the wounds properly," Drake said. "Make sure you guys die from each other's shots. It happens in gunfights all the time."

Unfortunately it did, Parker thought. And that was just too damn bad. It could work, but it would have to be done properly. His job now was to hold that off until the colonel arrived. "What about the two men we ID'd in the colonel's quarters?"

"Interesting. That's the problem with being out here at the airport most of the time," he spat out. "So what happened to those two?" Drake asked.

Parker shrugged. "I don't know. The men were taken away by Sergeant Hall."

A funny light came into his gaze. "Well, that's good," he said. "That's very good."

Parker frowned, not liking that. "Why is that?"

The gunman gave him a grim smile. "None of your business," he said. "You've been enough trouble already."

"We didn't want any trouble," Sandy said, a plea entering her tone. "We came to pick up our brothers. And to go home and bury them."

Drake shrugged. "I understand that, but you got yourself mixed up in a shitload more trouble."

"You could just let us go," she said, a note of desperation this time.

Parker squeezed her fingers as he tried to figure out where the hell Samson was. If this guy had shot Samson, that was seriously bad news. Another animal that needed a second chance. But so did Sandy. All of them did.

They were leaving this life to find another life outside of the military, and to think that this asshole was looking at taking it away from them. Well, that wasn't happening. Parker shifted his position, and the gun swung in his direction.

"You could let her go," Parker said. "She doesn't know anything. She's not part of this."

"Well, she is part of it now, isn't she?" Drake said. "I get you trying to save your little girlfriend here. But she's collateral damage."

At that, Sandy stiffened. "Collateral damage?" she cried out. "Are you serious? My life is so much more than that."

"Your life might have been, but your death isn't. You're in the wrong place at the wrong time. So sorry."

"I'm pretty sure you don't want to shoot us all in here," Parker said. "Just think of how obvious that'll look."

"Not when it's you doing the shooting," he said and motioned at the unconscious man.

"But he's unconscious still, and you know that forensics will be able to tell how old his wounds were, and you'll end up screwed."

"He needs to wake up soon," Drake said. "And, yes, I know all kinds of shit about forensics too. Thanks very much."

"Then you should try to wake him," Sandy said. "That'll be the first thing."

He stared at her, but there was a question in his eyes as he contemplated that. He walked over, still holding the gun on Parker, turned on the tap from one of the sinks into a big bucket of water but never gave them a chance to actually move. Parker shifted again, and Drake looked at him. But Parker had seen enough. Samson was behind Drake. But all Parker could see was his nose on the glass door in the office behind Drake.

Damn. Drake probably had put Samson in there on purpose.

They were just outside the office, and Samson was lying just inside. He couldn't even get out because the door was closed. Parker glanced around to see if there was any way to help open it so Samson could get out and add to the fray.

His opportunity would be when Drake tossed the water on Gregg. Drake would need two hands in order to make that happen. Parker waited quietly for the right moment. All around was nothing but silence. Vehicles should be coming soon. There should be a crew coming to take out the bad guys. So where was everybody?

"Did you set up our trip back supposedly leaving early on your own?"

Drake shook his head. "No. Gregg did. It was a combined effort actually," he corrected. Maybe he was afraid he wouldn't get his just rewards for that clever move.

"So, no pilot is coming?" he asked.

"Not for a few hours yet."

Parker glanced at Sandy to see the hope diminishing in her gaze. Again he squeezed her fingers and gave a subtle shake of his head, trying to get her to realize they weren't out of options yet. Not that he had any idea what those options would be, but he'd take a couple bullets before he let this guy go after her.

And Drake would have to be damn accurate or have very good luck in order to stop Parker with one bullet.

He tensed as the gunman came back holding the bucket, trying to tilt it with the handle, but the bucket kept shifting with the water to stay level. Finally, in frustration, Drake said, "Don't move." He tilted the bucket of water with both hands, the gun still in one hand, and dumped the water over Corporal Gregg's face.

In a sudden move, Parker jumped backward and kicked his foot out, opening up the office door. Samson bolted forward, growling. He jumped high and grabbed for Drake's firearm, and the man screamed. His gun fired once and then twice, as he tried to get the dog off him.

Sandy bolted back for the office and hid behind the wall as Parker bolted forward. And he took out the gunman with several hard chops to the jaw. It surprised him that it took three uppercuts. This guy had jaws of steel. Finally the gunman collapsed to the floor, Samson still growling.

Corporal Gregg, wet and barely conscious, was trying to get up on his hands and knees, struggling to decipher what the hell was going on. He ordered, "Samson down."

Samson let go and whined. He sat up and cuddled the dog, then turned to Parker with a smile.

Parker knew he was in deep shit. "Samson! Come here."

And caught sight of something unexpected.

Bang.

Corporal Gregg went down with a hard *thump*. Samson whined.

Parker called him over. "Come, Samson. Good boy."

Samson came running to him and sat down beside him.

Parker turned his gaze to Sandy, standing in front of him and a long way from the open office doorway where she'd come from, holding a small metal toolbox she'd clunked Corporal Gregg over the head with. He grinned and said, "Aren't you a handy person to have around."

She stood, shaking, tears in her eyes. He bolted to his feet and, with Samson at his side, he wrapped his arms around her. "We'll be fine. Take it easy."

"I want these men to never wake up," she cried out.

"I get that," he said. "Never waking up is one thing. Let's make sure they can't get free again." He handed her the gun. "Shoot them in the knees if they move. At this point, we can't take any more chances."

She stared at him in shock.

He nodded. "I know it's not what you do. But we'll

make sure they can't recover to attack us again." He walked around the mechanic's shop, finding some lightweight chains, some bungee cords and some rope. He came back, dropped the whole lot and secured both men back to back with their hands above their heads. They were strung together and weren't going anywhere.

Sandy said, "Could you, for good measure, wrap that chain around their waists?"

Parker looked at her in surprise and then grinned. "Are you hoping to drop them into an ocean somewhere?"

"I wish," she replied with a small smile, but he could see the tremors still racking her frame.

"All right," he said. "Just for you."

It took a lot of effort to slide the chain first under one and then under the other, but soon enough he had it done. He said, "You want me to put a lock on him too?"

She found a great big lock and gave it to him. "And hopefully they don't have a key."

He started to laugh. "You have a vindictive streak."

"I'll have nightmares for the rest of my life," she said. "I want this over with, and I want it over with now."

He nodded, and, with the men now fully secured, he knew she was more important than getting the news out and took her in his arms. He put the gun down on the desk and held her close.

She shuddered several times and then, with a great big sigh working up her chest and finally getting out, she sagged against him. "Oh, my God," she said. "I was so scared when he came back in. I thought you were out there to check on him, and then he was there in front of me, and you weren't. I was so afraid he'd killed you."

"*Shh*," he whispered. "I'm fine. You're fine. We made it

yet again."

"But for how long?" she asked, her tone somber. She twisted her head back and up to look at him. "How many times can we escape death?"

"I suggest we never get back into a position where we have to," he said gently, stroking her cheek. "Honestly this has been a pretty rough ride, but it will end."

She shook her head. "Not fast enough. What was that about our flights having been changed?"

"Only that we thought bringing us here early meant we were leaving early. But we weren't. Our flight is still on time."

She sagged. "Please tell me that we're not staying here with those two until then? Not alone."

"It'll be fine." He pulled out his phone. "Let me get this out."

She smiled and said, "Are you contacting the colonel himself this time?"

"I would if I thought it was the colonel's number, but I'm afraid we're still not done yet."

She stiffened and cried out, "What?"

He nodded. "Let me call Badger." He took a few steps away from her.

When Badger answered, sleepy, as if he'd just woken up or maybe had been enjoying the fruits of having a loving partner, Parker said, "This shit keeps going downhill."

CHAPTER 10

S ANDY LISTENED TO the conversation. Getting the gist
from a one-sided conversation took a bit. What she did
understand was that Parker wanted Badger to contact
Commander Cross again. Parker would use the other lines,
but he had no way of knowing if they were being tracked.
"And I'll tell you why ..."

She understood he thought somebody else was involved,
but she didn't want to contemplate such a horrific thing.

Finally he hung up the phone and smiled. "There is a
fridge with cold water. Do you want some?"

She shook her head. "What if it's poisonous?" She saw
his grin and glared at him. "I've been through too much,"
she cried out. "I don't trust anything or anyone. And don't
make fun of me."

"I'd never do that," he said, holding out the bottle. "It's
got a seal on it."

She inspected it closely, looking for any pinpricks in the
seal, and then broke the seal herself and popped off the lid.
She nodded. "All our water outside is dead hot now, isn't it?"

"Yes." Parker's phone rang. He answered. His eyebrows
shot up, and he said, "Colonel Barek, sir. Yes, thank you for
contacting me directly." And he hesitated and said, "I hate to
ask this, sir, but I believe there is a code word."

Her mouth dropped open in stunned silence. It took a

lot of audacity to ask a colonel to hand out his code word.

Parker continued to talk, although it seemed to be more like encrypted code than anything. When he hung up the phone, she asked, "Is the cavalry finally coming?"

He nodded. "They will be, in about fifteen minutes."

She moaned with joy and said, "Please let me get back stateside healthy. This is beyond ridiculous."

"I know," he whispered. He sat down beside her so they could watch the two men. Parker snapped his fingers, and Samson came running, obviously perturbed emotionally by what was going on. "This is hard on Samson too."

Sandy felt bad. How selfish she was being. She shifted and called Samson in between the two of them. He came willingly and dropped his head on her lap, but his gaze kept going to Gregg. She scratched him gently. "It's really hard when people misbehave," she said, "but it's worse when it's the ones we love."

"Always the worst," Parker said beside her. He gently stroked Samson's back. "I can see how emotionally difficult this is. He's partially bonded with us, but his main bond was with Gregg. And now he's confused."

"There's no way we can let him go," she said. "Not to another family. Not to somebody else. Every time he'll get a little more damaged."

"I don't know about that," Parker said. "But I do agree he's better off staying with us. And I guess by *us* that means *me*."

"Maybe." She nodded slowly. "I'd like to be in his life too."

He looked over at her, his fingers sliding down her fingers. "Just *his* life?"

She smiled. "Well, you too," she teased. "It's pretty hard

to let go of a bonding event like this."

"It does tend to make people come closer or tear them apart. They bond through something like this, or they don't want the reminder of seeing the other person all the time."

"Actually that makes a lot of sense," she murmured. "But, before all this mess, I liked you anyway."

His grin widened. "And since we're both free ..." he said, letting his voice trail off.

"We should spend some time getting to know each other a little better," she said with a nod. "Not to mention you know it'd be very good for Samson's mental health if we were to do that."

He chuckled. "That's what is important. We'll spend time together for the dog's sake." And he burst out laughing. She punched him lightly. He sobered and grinned. "So we should take several steps in that direction for his mental health ... and ours."

"Personally I thought we'd already taken many steps in that direction," she said with a wry smile. "It's hard to not like somebody who saves your life."

"Ditto," he said, tilting his head toward her.

"Oh, right," she said. And then she chuckled. "That we can even find something to laugh about in this place is amazing."

"It'll get chaotic when all hell breaks loose again," he whispered. "So just keep that sense of humor and realize we will get through this."

"Are they taking us back to the main part of the base again?"

He nodded. "We still have a few hours now, so most likely. Not to mention you want a coffee and a doughnut."

She shook her head. "I would much rather be home and

have that coffee and a doughnut. There's this little place called Tony something. I'm sorry. I'm drawing a blank."

"Tony's Treats," he supplied. "You're right. Best doughnuts ever."

"So, we can meet there, and I think we can even sit outside and have Samson with us," she said.

"It's a date."

"That'll seem awfully tame," she said. "We've had mad gunmen after us, all kinds of stuff to entertain us. Maybe the relationship would be boring after this."

He squeezed her fingers and said, "I'm pretty sure we can find lots of excitement to keep ourselves entertained."

She smiled and said, "Don't look now, but vehicles are coming."

He nodded slowly. "I heard them. Once they get here, the gong show is about to begin again. Are you ready?"

"Hell, no," she said. "But I do want to see these men carted away. I'm just afraid it'll be the wrong men."

"Exactly," his voice crept up. "I'm expecting to see the last traitor come through these open doors."

She looked at him in horror. "No! That's why you made all those phone calls, so he is picked up on the base and put away, without us ever having to see him again."

"I know," he said. "In theory that would work fine, but it's all about proof when a man is accused of being involved in something like this. You have to have evidence. You can't just let him walk."

She scrambled to her feet, Samson scrambling with her. "Does that mean we're heading into danger again?"

"Do you hear the vehicles? This isn't over, but we should be safe."

She snorted at that. "No," she said. "I highly doubt it.

But we can hope for that." She glanced down at the two men and said, "I really want to kick them."

He chuckled. "But they're down, tied up and can't move, so that's not fair. But I do understand the sentiment." As he checked both men for pulses, one of them opened his eyes and said, "You won't get away with this."

"Such a trite statement, Gregg," Sandy snapped. "Couldn't you come up with anything better?"

He glared at her. "You're a dead woman."

She kicked him in the head, smiling, then turned to Parker to say, "He was awake."

Parker squeezed her hand and spoke to Gregg, still wincing from her kick. "Actually," Parker said, "by the time the military is done with you, I suspect that death will be your end."

Gregg closed his eyes and didn't answer.

Holding Sandy's hand, Parker led her to the window near the main door, where they watched three vehicles come in and line up beside each other in front of the hangar. He hit the automatic button and opened the big doors.

"Are you sure you want to do that?" she asked.

The men were already hopping out the vehicles.

"They're not coming out with rifles," he said.

"No. But what if there are six more men coming?" She gasped as she recognized one of the men. "The colonel came himself!"

Parker nodded. "Yes, that was part of my request."

"He won't like you yanking his chain," she said.

He laughed. "I'm not yanking his chain. I'm cleaning his house. He should be *thanking* me."

"I think he thought you had done enough," she replied. "And that *he'd* cleaned his house."

"Well, as we can see, that was not the case." He walked over to stand beside the two men tied up.

As the six men approached, their gazes went from the men on the ground to him. And their gazes stayed on Parker.

The colonel stepped forward. "Parker?"

"Yes, sir."

"You need to work on how you secure your prisoners."

Parker grinned. "I think some of that you can be put down to Sandy. She wanted to make sure these suckers didn't get up again. I was all for putting a bullet in their knees. But she is a nurse ..." he said apologetically. At his words, all the men turned to her.

She took a half step closer to Parker and glared at them defiantly. "Pardon me," she said a little sarcastically, "if I don't seem too friendly. Since my arrival last night, I've been met with nothing but men trying to hurt me. US Navy men mostly and some local rebels. And if there's a head wound on this guy, it's because I hit him with the toolbox to knock him out while he was trying to shoot Parker and then trying to get Samson to attack Parker. Plus the kick to the head I gave him later when he told me that I was a dead woman."

The colonel tilted his head as he heard the threat, then smiled at her. "The military will be losing an excellent nurse. We thank you for all your assistance while you've been here."

"I just want to go home safe and sound. And, as much as I want to believe this is over, I somehow don't think it is."

"It is," the sergeant said, walking toward her. He stepped beside the two men and shook his head as he stared down at them.

Parker dropped her hand, as if to step around and look too. He motioned at her, speaking softly. "Go over to the colonel. I'm sure he's happy to let you sit in one of the vehicles."

She took several hesitant steps forward, not sure what she heard.

And then he urged her to hurry.

She broke into a run toward the colonel as Sergeant Hall pulled out a weapon. He held it, facing the colonel.

"Samson," Parker snapped.

Samson, still confused and slightly disoriented by the swift change in handlers, understood one thing though. "Attack," Parker snapped.

Sandy turned around to see Parker lunge for the gun arm of the sergeant.

Only he turned his aim to target Samson ...

Sandy cried out, "No." That was all it would take—one shot. And Samson would be no more.

And then she heard it.

Pop.

EVEN MOVING AS fast as he could, Parker couldn't reach the dog in time. He kicked, catching Hall behind his knee. And Samson, with his heart as big as anything, was still a direct target. But when that shot had gone off, Parker had almost lost his footing, thinking poor Samson had taken the bullet.

But his kick had jerked Hall's arm. And Hall's shot had gone wide. Samson landed and lunged again. And Parker was on Hall too. Not just Parker but several other men who had come with the colonel were in the fray.

Parker didn't know why it ended, but, all of a sudden, there was silence. And Hall was on the ground unconscious. Beside the other two captives.

Samson whimpered. Parker dropped to his knees and asked, "Are you okay, boy?"

Blood ran along Samson's side, but, as far as Parker could see, it was only a burn. He wrapped his arms around the dog, and Samson put his head under his arm, still trembling. The two just sat there.

But it wasn't just the two of them, it was now three. Sandy had wrapped them up in her arms. He pressed his head gently against her shoulder and whispered, "Can we go home now?"

She reached out and hit him on the shoulder. "You could have warned me," she cried out.

"I wasn't sure if he would make a move or not. The smartest thing would have been if he had stayed quiet," he said. "But I guess that was too hard for him to do."

The colonel spoke up then. "I think he figured that staying quiet wouldn't do him any good. In this way, he could either go out in a blaze of glory and take out as many of us as he could and maybe still get away with it or potentially free his friends, and they could disappear."

"Is it really possible to disappear anymore?" Sandy asked, her voice louder than normal. "For crying out loud, look at the world now."

The colonel nodded, his face sad. He motioned his arms wide around them. "Rebels, insurgents, mercenaries are everywhere we look. All a soldier has to do is step out of service and become a private hitman. They'd have no problem finding work."

Parker knew the truth behind that. He had seen it happen time and time again. "But not this time," he said, standing up slowly, keeping a hand on Samson. "Although I think Samson is a very confused dog at this point."

"I think Samson will have a fine life at this point," the colonel said, watching the dog. "You were so concerned about him that you pulled him out of the line of fire. That shows a caring and compassionate nature we don't often see."

"If it had been targeted at anybody else, I would have done the same. But Samson's already saved us several times. I didn't want this time to be his last."

The colonel stood, looked at his other men, and said, "Thanks for stepping in."

"Honestly we were just here to clean up the mess," one of them said, reaching out a hand to Parker to shake.

"I feel like I've done nothing but put these guys down. Now if only they'd stay down." Parker ran his fingers through his hair, turned back to the colonel and asked, "Now what do we do?"

His face was grim. "We now have five men in custody. Do you think we're done?"

"I think now that we've picked up Hall," Parker said, "chances are you're pretty well there. There might be one or two in the supply chain, and that's always a concern. But that's for you to sort out. I'm sure that anybody who is part of this will try to lay low. The chances of getting caught and having their lives changed forever are too great right now."

"Maybe," Sandy said, her spirit returning. "We have yet to get back stateside."

"And I'm sorry," the colonel said, "but I have to push your flights back."

She groaned out loud. "Seriously?"

The colonel nodded. "I do need all this documented and forensics done. So the airport just became closed for the next few hours. Might have to route you though Germany even then. Our planes are being rerouted to another base as it is. So I only have a smaller one to send you in."

"Can you delay it just a little bit?" she asked hopefully.

Parker laughed and wrapped an arm around her shoulders. "We should be good to stay a few more hours. Maybe even dinner is included this time."

"I'd say so," the colonel said. He turned to the rest of the men. "Get the crews out here."

And, with that, organized chaos ensued. The colonel motioned Parker and Sandy toward him. Samson came with them. The colonel said, "You were supposed to depart at nineteen hundred, but let's push that back to twenty-two hundred. We'll try to get it all done by then. That way you can sleep on the flight. At least a few hours."

"I'm good with that," Sandy said with a heartfelt expression. "I'd really appreciate it if we could get away today."

"Me too," the colonel said. "Let's see if we can make that happen. In the meantime, I want you to head back into the main part of the base. You've got a few hours here now."

She groaned. "We don't even have a place to wait in."

"We'll fix that too." He called one of the men over and said, "Corporal Pearson here will take you back."

They nodded, and, with Corporal Pearson leading the way, they grabbed their bags and hopped into one of the vehicles. Samson joined them without the cage. They headed back to the main barracks.

"Can you believe it?" Sandy said. "We're heading back there again."

"Hopefully for the last time," Parker said lightly. "This should be good now."

She smiled up at him. "Says you."

"But it does accent the fact that poor Samson here needs

us," he said in a droll voice. "And I don't think a date at Tony's will be enough."

"What are you suggesting?" she asked, snuggling up close.

He wrapped his arm around her and pulled her close. "We should sit like this for the next five hours," he said. "Because there's really no privacy for us to do anything more than that ..."

She chuckled. "How like a man. Right to the basics."

"Hey! Maybe I was talking about falling asleep."

"Well, ... you were talking about something, but it sure didn't have sleep involved," she said teasingly. "Besides, I wouldn't want to start something like that until we're back home again."

"What do you have to do when you get home?" he asked.

"I'm off until after the funeral," she replied. "Which, in my case, is a cremation and a celebration of life next Thursday. I go to work Monday."

"I suggest we spend as many minutes of the next week as we can together," Parker said. "By next Thursday, I will be officially unemployed."

Her eyes opened wide to that. "Wow," she said. "That's right. I've only got a week afterward anyway."

"Right? We have brand new lives starting. So how about we start them together?"

She smiled. "You know what? That sounds like a perfect start to me."

"But we have to get through today, and that means a million more questions."

She groaned. "That's why he wanted us to go back, isn't it? So we could give our statements."

"And potentially why the flight has been pushed back too." As they arrived back at the base, they were led right back to the colonel's office. They were asked to take a seat and were offered coffee, tea or water.

Sandy said, "Coffee, please, and if a doughnut is lying around, I won't say no to it. I need the sugar hit."

Parker laughed at her. "At least you have your voice again."

"I never lost it," she said. "I want to do whatever needs to be done to get out of here. I just can't believe how much we've been through already."

"Understood," he said. "I wonder how long until the colonel arrives."

"Maybe it won't be him. Maybe somebody else will deal with us."

"I think it'll be him and somebody else," Parker said.

Ten minutes later somebody finally arrived. "At ease," the colonel said as he entered his office with another officer, carrying a tray with coffee. The colonel said, "I hope one of those are for me."

"No, sir. I'll go get more," the soldier said. He placed the tray down on the desk for Sandy and Parker, removed the items and quickly disappeared with the empty tray.

Sandy stared at the heap of doughnuts and grinned. "At least he took me seriously."

The colonel motioned at the treats. "Which one of you needs a sugar fix?"

"Me," she said. "My energy is dropping quickly." She grabbed a cup of coffee and the top doughnut and sat back. "Glad to see you made it back safe, sir."

"Me too," he said. "I gather you guys thought many times today you wouldn't make it."

"I've seen action many times," Parker said, his voice quiet. "I just never expected to have to face it against my own men."

The colonel sat down with a heavy *thud*. "That's the biggest betrayal of all, isn't it? I sit here commanding thousands of men every day. And you see shit like that happening under your nose and wonder what kind of people would sell out their country and their souls for a few thousand bucks, take a life for even less than that, take multiple lives just to gain their freedom. All the while knowing that, in the end, they still won't get away scot-free. How absolutely despicable all of it is." He looked tired, fed up.

"I do want to thank you for not getting mad at the methodology I used to contact you," Parker said. "I did suspect Sergeant Hall a while back, and I wasn't sure if he was monitoring your calls or not."

The colonel looked at Parker in surprise. "Did you really?" He twisted a pencil in his hand as he thought back over the different events. "It'll take me time to get my mind wrapped around all the things he did have access to. But you're right. He often does monitor the calls, so, if you called for help, he would have come, but then, of course, I wouldn't have come too. I guess I owe Commander Cross a thank-you for this," the colonel said.

"I think Commander Cross's only wish is that Samson gets a decent home," Parker added.

"Hopefully you can sort this out now, sir," Sandy said around bites of a doughnut. "Parker, do you want one? They are delicious."

Parker watched her eat, her tongue licking the sugar off her lips, and he turned his attention to his own cup of coffee.

"Why not?" He reached for the largest one on the plate.

As he started eating, the colonel nodded his head at him. "You've been a huge asset. Are you sure you want to leave?"

Parker's eyebrows rose. "The decision was made with my brother's death," he said quietly. "It hasn't been easy."

"I know," the commander said. "I'd be more than happy to switch you over to military police investigations," he said. "I know that carries a certain amount of cachet but also a certain stain to it. Because we're always policing our own, but you did yourself proud today, son. I'd be even more proud to have you join my regiment."

Parker felt the surprise almost as a blow to his gut. "I don't know what to say, sir."

"I don't want you to say yes or no right now," the colonel said. "I want you to go home, and I want you to bury your brother. I want you to take time to think about it, and then you contact me. It won't be a problem to get you back in again. And, no, you won't lose your seniority, benefits or anything else. We'll just put it down as an extended leave for the moment. Compassionate grounds leave, whatever we need to do while you think about it."

"That's very generous of you," Parker said slowly. "I'm really not too sure what to say. I was looking forward to working the family business with my father. I need to spend some time with him to sort this out."

"Understood," he said. "No pressure. Definitely no pressure. But, as I have just seen what I thought was a good man who turned out to be something he was not, I don't want to lose a good man who I see for myself is just that."

That was one of the highest compliments Parker had ever been paid. That it came from a senior officer made it extra powerful.

Sandy reached across, gripped his hand and said, "That's a very nice offer. He's right. Let's take our brothers home and deal with our grief and get over this *lovely* day we've had here and see what you want to do."

"I certainly won't jump to any decision," he said. "That much is for sure."

The colonel turned to the paperwork before him and said, "I am bringing in a couple investigators. I'll stay here the entire time. I will follow you both until you are on that plane and until the plane is in the air, to make sure you get away safely. The next couple hours could be uncomfortable. So prepare yourself. There will be a lot of questions."

CHAPTER 11

I T WAS A couple grueling hours, where Sandy and Parker kept tripping over each other with answers, remembering bits and pieces as they tried to state exactly what happened. It should have been simpler. Should have been clear-cut, but it wasn't.

By the time they were done, Sandy was exhausted. She wanted to curl up, close her eyes and crash for hours.

The colonel looked at his watch. "The main rush of dinner is over. I suggest we eat and then head to the airport."

She glanced at her watch in surprise. "It's twenty hundred hours," she cried out.

"It is, indeed," the investigator said, closing his folders, and smiled. "And you put in a very hard day. Your country appreciates it. You'll be in Germany in no time. And likely asleep the whole way."

Sandy didn't know what to say to that. The country might appreciate it, but she was exhausted. The colonel and the investigator were right that she would sleep all the way home. But first she needed more food, real food.

She stood on shaky legs, and Samson stood up immediately. She looked down at him. "We lost the food we left at the airport, and once again he has no dog food."

"I'm pretty sure Samson's got a steak coming," the colonel said. "Let's go."

But instead of heading to mess hall, they were in the colonel's private room with a table. The room was empty of other people, and there was just them.

The colonel sat down at one side, and Sandy and Parker took places on the other side. Instead of walking to the self-serve cafeteria, they were being served. When the waiter came to ask what she would like with her steak, she told him a huge Caesar salad, a massive baked potato and all the trimmings.

Parker chuckled. "Make that two servings of everything," he said. "We're very hungry. Add an extra steak for Samson, please."

The colonel made it three orders. He also brought out some wine. "It's a special occasion," he said. "I don't have a problem having a drink. And, if it helps you to sleep on the way back, all the better."

The next forty-five minutes were one of the most pleasant dinners she'd experienced. They talked about everything from dog breeds to cutting-edge nursing techniques to the colonel's own two sons, both of whom were professionals—one an engineer and one a medical doctor.

Samson gobbled a chopped-up steak and cooked yams and lay at their feet.

Sandy smiled at the colonel. "You must be very proud of your sons."

"I am. Sometimes you don't understand where the paths will take you. I really wanted them to follow in my footsteps. But, if they had, they wouldn't be who they are. And who they are, I am damn proud to know and even prouder to call family. We can't push people to do what we think they should do because it's not right for them in our mind."

"Too bad so many other parents can't figure that out,"

Sandy said with a smile.

"Exactly." He nodded. "Neither of you are married, correct?"

"No," Parker replied. "Haven't even gotten close."

"I wonder where you will be in a year from now?" the colonel joked.

Sandy could feel the heat rising up her cheeks. Because it was the same thought that had flashed in her mind. She finished her steak, most of her baked potato and all of her salad. "Now I am stuffed," she said with a laugh.

"For a few hours," Parker teased.

She nodded. "Hopefully those few hours will be flying, and I'll be sleeping." She stretched her hand down and rubbed the top of Samson's head and smiled. "This guy has also had a hell of a couple days. I'm sure he is looking forward to some quiet time."

"A hell of a few months in his case," Parker corrected. "Just think of how many times he's been the saving force behind us."

She nodded and gave Samson a big hug. He threw his weight into her, letting her know he was not only happy to receive the physical affection but was craving it.

"He just needs some time, and he will be fine," the colonel said. "Maybe some training for you?" he asked Parker.

"Absolutely. I do want to keep him, and I think that's important for Samson. He's had a lot of different owners lately, and that's confusing."

The colonel stood and said, "A little bit of wine is left, if you want it?"

Sandy shook her head. "No. I'm good, thanks. I do appreciate that you brought us here and that we've had this evening to calm down. I can't wait to get to the airport, but, more than that, I just want to be in the air."

The colonel nodded and said, "Of course."

"My brother's cremation is in a few days, and that's a painful process which I want to get past. Saying goodbye is something I feel like, in a way, I've partially done from the ceremony you had today. It already seems like a long time ago after so much else has happened."

The colonel nodded and said, "Come on. Let's head out to my vehicle."

"Are the other family members around?"

"Not now. They are at their hotels in town, as they are taking commercial flights."

"Right," Sandy said. "For them, it's just been a chance to visit a base that they've probably never seen before."

"It's very different from most people's expectations. Only those of you who have actually done tours here have any true understanding."

"I'm sure this is just as painful for them as it is for us," Parker said. "We had the extra excitement, but, for them, it's still no less traumatic to be taking home a family member."

"Exactly." Outside, the colonel motioned to his jeep and said, "Hop in."

With Samson between them, they did. A driver came out, and Parker almost smiled at that. Sandy glanced at him, questioning. He just shook his head. But she realized, of course, the colonel didn't drive anywhere. As they drove out, she twisted to look behind them. "It's so hard," she said. "When you look back, I mean. I might never come here again."

"I know," Parker said, as he studied the area around them. "When we got off the plane, I just wanted to look for a dog as a distraction for my real reason to be here. I hadn't expected this at all."

She laughed. "When you offered me a chance to go for a ride, I wanted to get off the base, away from all the heavy memories. I can easily tell you that all those heavy memories have been parked firmly in place. I can see how my brother could have come up against the wrong bullet with his name on it instead of the IED that killed him. The violence we've seen since we've been here ..."

"Which is not normal," the colonel said. "You know that, right?"

"Yes," Sandy said. "It's not normal, but it did help maybe, and I guess it's wrong to say this, but it did help to put my brother's death in perspective."

"Then that would be a help that we hadn't even considered," the colonel said. "It's hard to lose loved ones. Grief is all-consuming, and then, all of a sudden, it's not. Sometimes we feel guilty, and sometimes we look for other things to fill our lives. Maybe this last day will have helped you deal with that."

"I'll still cry at the ceremony, and I'll still cry at odd times in my life, but I'm pretty sure I can see that he did what he loved and that he was joyous doing it. I'm just grateful it wasn't friendly fire that took him out."

"Exactly," the colonel said. The rest of the journey was done in silence.

It was getting dark out, and the headlights showed a completely different world that she hadn't seen before. It had been dark before, but now, heading back, knowing all the issues were done and gone, it had such a different feel to it.

Parker reached across Samson and clasped her hand in his. She smiled at him. "Is it safe this time, do you think?" she teased.

"Yes," he said. "It is. We just have to get through this next little bit."

"I'm trusting you," she said with a wink.

"Good," he said. "Keep trusting me because you've trusted me right from the beginning, and I've trusted you." He looked down at Samson, sitting between them, and asked, "How you doing, Samson?"

Samson gave a short bark.

"I hope his cage is still there at the airport," she said. "He needs it to be coming home with us."

"I hope so too," Parker said.

The colonel said from the front seat, "It was left behind on purpose."

Within another few minutes they arrived at the airport. They hopped out with their bags and walked over to where the cage stood.

The colonel reached out, shook Parker's hand. Parker saluted and watched as Sandy wrapped her arms around him and gave him a hug. He grinned, and she stepped away and said, "Thank you very much."

They opened the cage for Samson, and he went in willingly. He lay down, his eyes ever watchful.

It seemed to take longer than expected, but finally, with Samson securely tied in beside them, they each took seats and waited for the cargo hold to close.

This wasn't your average flight, but it was one they had taken themselves at different individual times. Sandy stared out at the darkness as the door finally closed.

She gripped Parker's fingers tighter.

"Here we go," he said.

"You know I'm okay with that," she said. "I'm definitely okay with that."

He laughed and whispered, "I suggest that, instead of us splitting up, we both go to one place."

"I agree. And … it should probably be my place," she said with a shy smile.

"Well. It is closer," he said. "Probably cleaner."

"Definitely cleaner," she said with a chuckle. She squeezed his fingers. "We still have a long-ass trip to go."

"In many ways," he said.

Something in his tone had her opening her eyes and turning to face him. "*In many ways?*"

He nodded. "In many ways. Because it's not just about getting home, it's also about the funerals. It's also getting to know each other. That's the journey I am looking forward to."

She smiled and said, "You say the nicest things."

"To the next chapter of our lives," he said and squeezed her fingers again.

"Sounds good to me."

A voice interrupted their eye-gazing, letting them know to buckle up. The engine started. And finally the plane turned and headed down the runway.

She couldn't wait. As soon as it took off into the air, she squeezed his fingers, lay her head back and closed her eyes. If there was one thing she could hope for, it was to sleep all the way home. Seconds later she could feel herself slipping under.

PARKER WOKE AFTER a very rough flight to hear the sounds of the engine changing. He glanced over to find Sandy curled up against his shoulder; even Samson was sound asleep in his crate.

He looked out the cockpit window and could see the lights below.

They were coming into Germany. He gave Sandy a gentle shake but still enough to make sure she woke up. "Pit stop."

"Are we staying here for a bit, or are we heading out right away?"

"I think it's a two-hour stop. Then on to stateside. We'll be joining another group too."

She nodded and yawned. "Good. I can't wait to get home," she murmured, nestling closer. "But even more I'm glad to have left there."

Parker smiled, wrapped an arm around her shoulders and tugged her closer. "Agreed." And he kissed her forehead.

Within twenty minutes they were standing and ready to disembark. He wanted to take Samson out of the crate, but that wasn't likely to be a good idea here. If Samson didn't walk himself, Parker would have to carry him or get a trolley. And that was not the way things were usually done. But, as he stepped off carrying Samson in his crate, he could see a long trolley set to the side. He placed the dog crate on it and wheeled it toward where they could wait for the next couple hours. But he needed to find a place to let the dog out to do his business. A whistle called out toward them. He looked over to see Gorman standing there with a big grin on his face. Parker didn't know the man himself but after Cam mentioning him, he'd looked him up as part of his research. The big German male was hard to miss.

Parker laughed, waved and turned to Sandy, standing right beside him and said, "That's Gorman. He must have recognized Samson."

"You want to go say hi?" she asked, yawning.

"We've got a wait anyway," he said. "It wouldn't hurt to wait with somebody."

He pushed Sampson over until they stood beside Gorman. "Hey. Cam told me I could find you here. I'm Parker. How you doing?" Parker asked.

"I'm doing great. Cam told me you were looking for me," he replied. "I'm about to head back to the base. I heard you were coming in with the dog. Quite a ruckus over on base, huh?"

"I know," Parker said. "It just wouldn't quit. They're still doing a full-on investigation as to everybody connected. Good thing you're not there. All kinds of crazy going on."

"Unfortunately," Gorman said, "I will be there soon." He pointed out his big duffel bag beside him. "I'll be out in an hour or so."

"Right. Well, we get to go home finally."

"Along with a coffin. Sorry about that. That's got to be a hard trip."

"It is for both of us." Parker turned and introduced Sandy. "We both have had a rough trip."

The two shook hands, and then Sandy stepped closer, leaning in, and said, "I know I need to stay awake so I can sleep on the next flight, but it's hard."

"You want to come around in the back here?" Gorman asked. "There's a place where you can sit down. We can get a cup of coffee."

Parker brightened up. "Sounds good." He looked at Sandy and asked, "Are you up for it?"

"Both big yeses. Sitting and coffee." They walked and talked at the same time, following Gorman, pushing Samson with them.

A few minutes later Parker looked around and said, "And where exactly are we going for this coffee?"

"By the time we get there, we'll have to turn around and come back to catch the next flight," Sandy joked.

The blow came out of nowhere. Parker sank to his knees, his mind and body still grasping what had just happened when he heard Sandy cry out. And then silence.

He lay on his side, crumpled to the ground, watching as two men stood there arguing. It was Gorman and his buddy, Tobey Manfred. Samson barked like crazy inside his cage. The cage was right in front of Parker, if only he could find a way to open that latch.

Gorman turned around and kicked the cage hard. And that just set Samson off more. "I think we should pop the dog," he said.

"And deep-six these bodies. Somewhere. Make sure they are never found. Make it look like a psychopath found them," his buddy said.

"I like the idea of *never being found.* It'll look like they walked off the base and never showed up again."

"You got any idea where that can be?"

"Yes," Gorman said. "I think so. But we have to get him out of here, and we have to get him out of here fast."

Samson was still going crazy, and Gorman kicked the cage again.

This time putting it almost within Parker's reach.

"Shut the fuck up," he roared. "God, I hate that dog." Another kick followed.

This time the cage came within reach. Parker snuck his hand out and slowly worked the cage around where he flipped open the latch. With one hard effort, he spoke to Samson. "Attack." And popped open the end hatch.

Samson bolted from the edge of the crate and raced toward Gorman, lunging before Gorman even had a chance to react.

At the same time, Parker was up on his feet and dove toward the other man's legs. He took him down and removed his weapon. In the next move, he turned and fired at Gorman, taking out his kneecap. Gorman screamed and went down.

The man under Parker managed to flip Parker over onto his back. Parker still held the weapon, and he shoved it hard against the man's shoulder and said, "Just make one move, I'll be more than happy to blow your shoulder joint apart. See if you ever get to use that arm again."

The guy slowly settled back, pushing his hands up.

"Yeah, you better hold up your hands," Parker said, right before he clubbed him with the handle end of his gun.

Tobey had been silenced, while Gorman continued to cry out.

Parker crawled to his knees and then upright, hating the wooziness from the blow to his head. He'd been clocked hard. He backed up several steps and crouched beside Sandy. She moaned. "Take it easy, Sandy," he whispered. "But if you can wake up now, that would be a huge help."

"I'm awake," she said. "What happened?"

"We got blindsided by Gorman and his buddy. I'm assuming they are part of this whole export-of-stolen-military-goods thing. Perhaps that's why they are in Germany."

"But nobody knew," she said, struggling to her feet, "until now."

Parker helped her upright. "Take it easy. We need to handle these two guys." He looked over to see Samson, his jaw locked on the other man's shoulder. Parker hadn't called off Samson. Parker hesitated to do so. Because, once again, that would give Gorman a chance to fight back. But Samson could also guard the other man too. "Samson, release."

Samson growled.

"Samson, release." He made his voice calm and authoritative. Almost immediately Samson let go, backed up and looked at Parker.

He walked over and said, "Samson, guard." And he pointed to both men.

Samson shifted ever-so-slightly and sat down, looking at them.

Parker turned to look at Gorman and said, "You're not going anywhere for a very long time. That knee is permanently buggered as far as I'm concerned. Your buddy here might try to take me out when he comes to, but, since I've got his weapon, I won't hesitate to blow him apart too."

He tossed his phone to Sandy and said, "Badger is at the top of that list. You might want to call him."

She stared at him and then dialed Badger's number, putting the phone on Speaker. "Badger, you're on Speaker."

She walked closer to where Parker was, so he could speak. "Badger, I'm holding two guys, Gorman, and his buddy Tobey Manfred. They attacked us at the base in Germany on our two-hour layover. They were part of the military supplies thefts. But I don't have a clue who here to talk to. So I'm back to contacting you."

"Stand tight," Badger said. "I'll have help in minutes."

Parker motioned at Tobey, who had come to, and said, "Roll over onto your stomach."

The guy curled his lip.

"I'll sic Samson on you, or I'll blow your kneecap apart, or I'll do both," Parker said, his voice harsh. "I am so done with this that I'd put one in your head if I didn't think it would get me in trouble. But I have no problem riddling your body with bullet holes and taking out major joints."

The man rolled over slowly.

Parker looked to see if they could secure them with anything.

Sandy shrugged. "Let's take off their shoelaces from their big work boots."

With Parker holding the gun first on Gorman, still moaning and crying out about his knee, then on Tobey, as they untied the laces on their boots and secured them both.

Finally feeling a little better, Parker stepped back out of sight at the sound of a vehicle racing toward them. He looked over at Sandy and said, "Be ready."

"Are they friends or foe?"

"It seems like we're pretty damned even on this trip. I don't trust anybody anymore."

"Gotcha," she said.

"Step back behind me while I have the weapon," Parker urged her.

She didn't waste any time and stepped behind him. She could still see but was no longer front and center.

Not just one vehicle came. There were three. Gravel sprayed as the trucks came to a hard stop. Parker kept his weapon on the prisoners.

"Stand down, young man."

"Identify yourself," Parker said.

"I will. But you've got to drop that weapon."

Parker slowly lowered it. "We've been attacked more than enough today," he said. "We're done being vulnerable. I am not giving up this weapon. Not for one fricking moment. Not until you properly ID yourself."

One of the men stepped forward. "Commander Cross sent us. Now lower your weapon, soldier." At that magical name, Parker relaxed and handed over the weapon.

CHAPTER 12

S ANDY WAS NEVER leaving home again. She sighed. Not only that, she couldn't let go of Parker's hand either. The two of them clung together through the questioning, refreshments, coffee until they were finally allowed to get on board the plane to the States.

Even on board, they hardly spoke; they just continued to cling to each other. Or maybe it was she who clung to him. To think that they'd been attacked yet again ... She didn't understand why Gorman would take the chance of accosting them. Nobody even considered that he was involved. At least she hadn't. Of course it was quite possible that throughout the investigation his and his friend's names would come up.

Gorman and Tobey had been at the airport when the dog first went missing. With Ronnie opening the dog's cage, was that the diversionary tactic that he'd needed? Every time she closed her eyes, she kept seeing friends turned to strangers turned to enemies and killers. It was like blows coming out of nowhere—full of deceit and betrayal.

As soon as she'd open her eyes, she'd find herself covered in a film of sweat. She wondered how long it would take to get over something like this. The last thing she wanted from this trip was PTSD. And yet, since her arrival, it had been nothing but hell.

The German base colonel had looked at the two prisoners as if they were dirt that had sullied his home. The men would be dealt with unceremoniously. She had no idea what would happen to them long-term and didn't care, as long as they weren't set free again. They were assholes of the first order.

"Can't sleep?"

Sandy shook her head and whispered, "Maybe never again." She snuggled in as he shifted to the side, so she could curl up against him.

"Nothing else will happen," he said, his voice calm. "I promise."

"What if somebody else in that bloody nightmare is waiting for us stateside?"

"I doubt it. There really wasn't anybody stateside to get involved. They were selling overseas."

"Maybe, but it's hard to be sure. We thought we were safe in Germany, and look what happened."

"I know. For that, I'm so damn sorry."

"It's not your fault," she said, yawning. "Not your fault in any way. It's just so shitty that it had to happen this way."

"I know, but just relax. Let it all go. We can get through this. We have a tough week ahead of us, but we don't have to be alone. We can do this together."

"That sounds lovely," she said. "You know I won't want you to leave when we get home. It seems like we've been together since forever."

"Me too," he murmured against her hair. He massaged the back of her neck. "Close your eyes," he ordered. "Just sleep."

She was so tired, yet she wanted to laugh at his command because sleep was hardly something you turned off and on like that. But she was seriously too tired to even bother.

She was also terrified of closing her eyes and seeing all those scenes happen over and over again. As Parker gently stroked the back of her neck, she could feel herself letting some of the tension fall away, and her stress eased. "How much longer do we have?" she murmured.

"About four hours," he said. "Four hours and we will be home. Soon we'll be in Coronado, and it will seem like we never left."

"Oh, I don't know," she said. "It's been a pretty shitty trip. Hard to forget."

"Ditto," he said. But he continued to work the muscles at the back of her neck and the top of her shoulders.

"Don't let me sleep too long," she murmured, feeling herself slipping under again. But once again the dreams caught hold of her and wouldn't let go. She was running and running but couldn't get away from those faceless men chasing her. Somewhere in there was Samson, jumping for throats and shoulders, taking down intruders and bad guys. Her arms wrapped around Parker, she held on tight. She could hear, even in her dream state, Parker's soothing voice saying, "Take it easy. Just rest. You're safe. Relax."

Her arms tightened convulsively. And then she slowly relaxed and slipped deeper. And finally she slept.

When she woke not long after, she felt marginally better. But that little bit of sleep had just reminded her how much sleep she'd actually been missing. She yawned, shifted her position, and asked, "Now how long?"

"We're almost there," Parker said. "Not to worry."

"Maybe," she said. "I just want to go home and be in my own bed."

Finally they landed. She was too tired to do much. More military trucks came to take the coffins. She was too tired, too dry-eyed, and too worn out to do much but stand here solemnly as they were loaded up. She was wrapped up in the circle of Parker's arms as he hugged her close.

When they finally pulled apart, she looked around and said, "Home—finally. Or almost home ..."

Once another trolley appeared to transport Samson in his crate, they were good to go.

"My truck is here. Come on." They went to the parking lot and found his truck. He helped her in the front, threw their bags into the back, then he lifted Samson into the truck bed and said, "I need your address so I can get you home."

She yawned, nodded, gave him her address and said, "I can't believe how tired I am. I'm just finished emotionally, physically ..." She let her voice trail off.

"Understood," he said. "You and me both." He drove off the base and over to her place.

Once they arrived, Sandy stepped out, looked up at her home and said, "Wow. It doesn't even feel like home."

"I know. Come on." He grabbed their bags.

She looked at him for a moment with their bags, then nodded. "Good," she said. "I wasn't thinking straight. Of course I should have invited you in."

"I don't really want to leave you alone right now," he said.

"I don't know what *your* reasoning is," she said, stifling yet another yawn, "but I don't want to leave you ever. It seems like we've been together since forever, and it feels so damn right."

They unloaded Samson from his crate, let him stretch his legs. He took care of his business and then excitedly followed them as they headed for the front door.

Sandy unlocked the door, pushed it open and stepped

inside. She looked around and said, "I can offer you the couch or my bed."

He stood for a long moment and stared at her.

She nodded again. "We'll put that down to me being too tired," she announced. She shut the front door, locked it and headed for her bedroom.

As she walked in, she kicked off her outer layer of clothing until she was in her panties and bra. "I am just going to collapse," she said. She pulled back one side of her bed linens, tucked under the covers and crashed.

PARKER STARED IN amusement as Sandy completely wiped out on him. Of course it was much better that she managed to get into bed on her own versus him having to help her. He followed suit, taking his clothes off a little more carefully, went into the bathroom and gave himself a scrub down as much as he could, then brushed his teeth and crawled into bed beside Sandy.

She rolled over and tucked up close.

"Perfect," he whispered. "You turn to me instinctively, just the way it should be." He placed a soft kiss on her head and pulled her tight against his body.

She mumbled incoherently and then her breathing evened out.

He fell asleep right behind her. His dreams were almost as troubled as hers seemed to have been. But, in each and every one, she was the one getting hurt, and he wasn't there in time to save her. When he finally woke the next morning, it was early. Somewhere around four o'clock, and dawn was just lighting up the sky. But it hadn't risen yet. He lay here for a long moment, wondering if sleep was something he could try for again. It was hours before the world would wake up, and he didn't have any place to go or to be today. Neither did Sandy. And what a joy that was.

Not to mention the time change and the jet lag and the adrenaline rush that left you so drained afterward …

They were finally back in California, with all the nightmares over with—at least the physical real-life ones—and he realized that, even if he could go back to sleep, what about poor Samson? Parker hopped out of bed and checked on the dog, who had taken over the couch. Samson lifted his head, wagged his tail and rolled over to show his belly, but that was the extent of it. Parker rubbed his belly and figured that maybe Samson was okay to sleep longer.

Parker went back to bed and curled in close against Sandy. Once again she snuggled into him, looking for him. He wrapped his arms around her and held her close. He whispered against her ear, "What a gift you are."

She again mumbled something unintelligible.

He chuckled. And that seemed to do it.

She leaned back slightly, opened her sleep-clouded eyes to stare up at him. "What's so funny?" she whispered.

He dropped a kiss on her nose, then her lips, and whispered, "You. You're so sleepy. Go back to sleep. I'm sorry I woke you."

"Well, now that you woke me up," she said, "don't waste the opportunity."

Not sure exactly what she meant by that, but hoping he did, he shifted so she lay flat on her back, his arms under her head. He kissed her nose, then her lips, her chin, and said, "I don't want to take away sleep from you."

"How about you replace it with something better?" she

said, shifting her body, still warm from sleep, and her voice still cloudy with dreams. She shifted her hands to slide through his hair and tugged him forward. "Like a reason for living," she whispered. "I think we saw enough of the negative side of life. How about we find joy in the good side of life?"

He wouldn't argue with that. His lips crushed hers, even as he held his weight up mostly off her body.

But she wasn't having any of that. She pulled him down lower, until he was crushing her.

"I'm too heavy," he whispered.

She shook her head. "No. You're just right." And she reached up and kissed him. This time she kissed him deep and thoroughly, leaving him wanting so much more. She murmured, "I might be still half asleep, but this is a perfect way to wake up." Kissing his cheeks and his chin and his nose, Sandy stroked his shoulders and his arms. "Did I ever say *thank you* for saving my life?"

"Did *I* ever say *thank you* for saving my life?" he murmured, dotting her lips with kisses.

Her tongue slid out to gently stroke his lips, tangling and warring with his.

He kissed her deeper. The passion rose between them as heated skin slid across heated skin, soft gasps and whispered murmurings flowed through the room as they caressed, teased and gently explored each other.

"I'm so grateful you were there with me," Sandy whispered.

"Me too," Parker murmured against her mouth, his hands going behind her back and unhooking her bra. She arched to give him more access. Within seconds he had the bra off and tossed to the floor. He smoothed his hands over her beautiful breasts, cupping, weighing, measuring, ... tasting ...

"They're so beautiful," he whispered, taking first one and then the other in his mouth as his fingers slid over her hips, stroking the inside of her thighs, along the back of her legs, across the top of the little scrap of lace, feeling her belly clench beneath him. His hand slid under the lace along the back to grip her cheek, and he squeezed gently.

She moaned, her hips restless already, pressing into his palm.

He pulled his head back, gasping. "Easy," he said. "Take it easy."

"No," she demanded. "I don't want it to be easy. I want you now."

He chuckled, quickly removing the scrap of lace and tossing it to the side.

Her hands went to his boxers, trying to pull them off. But he was down too far for her to reach.

He shifted so he could pull them off himself before returning to find her. Her legs were wide open, her body ready, waiting, anxious for him.

He slid into position, and she shook her head. "No waiting, no teasing," she said, reaching for him. "Come to me."

He kneeled between her thighs and thrust deep within her, already rising past the point of trying to prolong this. She clung to him. He thrust once, twice, and then they came apart, together. In each other's arms, they gasped and clung and rode the crest. It was incredible, quick and exactly what they needed right now. He whispered, "I'll take more time with you in our second go-round."

"Good to know. We will be doing this for the rest of our lives," she said, hooking her arms around his neck. "So we should start out the way we mean to go on."

He laughed and held her close. "Forever."

"Forever."

EPILOGUE

CADE SAT DOWN on the front steps of Geir's house and wiped the sweat off his face.

Geir sat down beside him. "You okay, man?"

"I am. Just thinking about those dogs. I can't believe what poor Parker and Samson went through. That's just insane. Here we thought this military dog was a perfect match for him in Iraq."

"They are all out safely now. We'll see a lot more of them too. Parker—and Sandy—are talking about relocating here to New Mexico. Parker did get offered a pretty sweet deal in Iraq but not sure he's looking at it seriously. I think losing his brother changed something for him. He wants to spend more time with his father before it's too late."

"That would be great," Cade said. "He's a good person."

"Samson will come, of course," Geir said. "It's amazing how many of our guys have ended up keeping the dogs."

"When the dog saves your life, there is that sense of gratitude and indebtedness, where you want to look after them and to make sure they have a decent life."

"I know, and what the heck are we doing about the next one?"

"You know what I was thinking about this morning?" Cade said. "Carter here." He motioned at the man standing with a tool belt around his hips, a two-by-four in his hand

and a pencil behind his ear. "He's been pining for his dogs back."

"What do you mean, *pining for his dogs back*?" Geir asked.

"He was married, then divorced, and his wife got to keep the dogs. They had a breeding pair of labs. Apparently he was really good with them, and he misses them a lot."

"But does he care about going after a K9 dog?" Geir asked. "It's hardly the same thing."

"No, it sure isn't the same thing. But he's wasted here."

"Hardly," Geir said. "He's been a huge help."

"He is, but he's also way more capable than this. He should have his own company."

They studied him and the prosthetic right hand that he worked completely carefree.

"So why doesn't he?"

"I think he's been struggling to find himself again."

"When did he get divorced?"

Cade nodded. "That's the question, isn't it? She walked out when he was in the hospital having multiple surgeries. Probably about the time she realized he could be missing multiple limbs."

"Bitch," Geir said.

"Easy to judge but this life's not for everyone."

"No, we're the blessed ones, aren't we?"

"We are," Cade said. "Now Carter here, I think there's a hell of a lot more he could do."

"But where?"

"His best buddy's in Montana. Been asking him to come to the ranch since his accident, but he's refused."

"But how good friends were they?"

"Went to school together. Carter used to take all his military leave and head there. And he always helped out on his buddy's ranch, but now Carter feels like he can't anymore, thinks he's not as able."

"So, what will we do? Send him up to Montana?"

"That's where the next dog is, right?"

Geir looked at him in shock. "Seriously?"

"Seriously. Not exactly sure what happened to the dog. The file is pretty blank. Apparently the dog disappeared. Supposed to have been adopted by a family in Montana, and, when the military checked up on the adopted family, they never received the dog. Now the family has moved on. Aren't interested in adopting him anymore, and the dog is still missing."

"Since how long?"

"Since four months," Cade said. "A bloody long time."

"When did they find out the dog was missing?"

"About a month later. But again, no time, no money, no man-hours."

"It'll be almost impossible to find a dog like that now," he said.

"Yes, and no," Cade said. "The adoptive family said they had been called about him a couple times but hadn't really kept any of the information as to who'd called. And they wanted the Department of Defense to leave them alone. They were extremely uncooperative, not forthcoming at all."

Silence reigned between them. "Do you think there's any chance they did something to the dog?" Geir asked. "Did something bad and then didn't know how to cover their tracks and said they never got him?"

Cade slid him a sideways look. "You and I both know that, at the heart, most people are good, but some don't quite make the grade. Do they?"

"But to hurt a War Dog? That would be really shitty. ... And maybe, just maybe, they didn't get him. Maybe they took one look at him and took off. What's this one called?"

"Matzuka. It's one of the names that I've always remembered. I was trying to find somebody in the Montana area, and I was talking to Carter here, and he's the one who told me that his best buddy was there. He wants to go and see him, but he isn't quite ready, or so he says."

"What kind of funding does he need to start up his own business?"

"Enough money to build his first house probably," Cade said. "Think about one hundred thousand, maybe? Maybe not even that much. But then I don't know if that's even what he wants. He's a dark horse, hard to read him." He frowned. "We really need to have some sort of a fund to help these guys."

"That's a lot of money to come up with though," Geir said.

"I'm not sure he's all that broke. I think he's here because he's lost, like so many of us were, and I think it's more a case of he needs a reason to go there. Just like the rest of them did."

"Does the best friend have a sister by any chance?"

Cade looked at him, and his gaze twinkled. "Are you up to more matchmaking?"

"Maybe," Geir said. "We're doing pretty damn good so far."

"Well, his friend does have a sister, but that doesn't mean anything's between them."

"No, but, if they aren't together, they can't become an item, can they?"

"I think there was some talk about the two of them not

getting along," Cade said. "It's one of the reasons why I've hesitated. What I don't want is to have Carter put in a situation where he feels obligated to stay and yet where he's not comfortable. Here he can be free and easy with us."

"He's hiding," Geir said bluntly. "And we all know exactly what that feels like. So do we call him over and ask him? Or ...?"

Cade nodded. "I was just waiting for the right time." He watched as Carter took off his tool belt, hitched it to the back of the pickup. He gave a whistle.

Carter looked at him and nodded.

"Here goes nothing," Cade said and hopped up. "I'll let you know how it works out."

"WELL, WELL, WELL," Brandon said, looking at Carter. "You're a sight for sore eyes."

The two exchanged hugs. Carter was self-conscious about his arm but slapped his buddy on the back of his shoulder. "Hey."

"That's it? Just a hey? I've been trying to get you to come out for what? ... Years? At least since you got blown up. And for some dang reason you walked away from the people closest to you."

"The one who was really closest to me," Carter said, "walked away from me first. She left me feeling isolated and wanting to keep it that way."

Brandon looked at him and smiled. "I can understand that. But then your wife was a first-class bitch. I told you that a long time ago."

Carter chuckled. "She was, indeed," he said. "And, yes,

you did. I ignored you, and we had a lot of good years. But ..."

"*But* is correct. Anyway, enough of her. Come on. Let's go." Brandon looked around for Carter's bags and frowned. "You only got the one bag?"

"I travel light these days," Carter said, picking up his bag. He didn't want his friend to think he needed help. He was still touchy on that subject.

They walked over to the truck, and Carter tossed his pack in the bed. He asked, "Is this a new rig?"

"Yep. Ranch is doing well."

Carter chuckled. "There are worse things in life."

"There are a lot of worse things in my life. Debbie moved out last week."

Carter stared at his buddy. "What? Why?" He shook his head. "You guys have been so close forever. You've been married like what? Ten years?"

"She thinks I had an affair," Brandon said abruptly.

"Did you?" Carter asked. They'd always had that kind of relationship where they could be up front and open.

Brandon shook his head. "No. I didn't. But I almost did."

"I think, for women, there is no *almost*," Carter said with a frown, his heart sinking. "As soon as you think about it, consider it, they know all too well that's where your body goes. Faithful doesn't mean just physical."

"I know. I was stupid, and I'm damn sorry, and I want her back, but she's not even talking to me."

"Shit," Carter said morosely. "That's not what I expected. I thought you two would be good forever."

"We would have been," Brandon said, "if I wasn't such a fool. There's more to it than that, ... but that's the gist of it.

Anyway, you will get to know all that lovely dirt on me as time goes by. What's this about a dog?"

"Yeah, it's probably a make-work reason to be here, but I figured it was time."

"Hell, yes, it's past time," Brandon snapped. "I don't know why you wouldn't come here to heal."

"Because you would have taken care of me, and you would have made it too easy to not get back on my feet," Carter said.

"I wouldn't treat you like a baby. I can always use real help on the place."

"Do you still have a bunch of hands helping out?"

"Sure do. More than when you were here last. Business is good, as I said."

"Any of them female?"

Brandon winced. "The new cook," he said. "Yes, she's gone too."

"Probably just not fast enough for Debbie, huh?"

"No, not fast enough. But it doesn't matter how many times I say I was a fool, and nothing happened, she still doesn't believe me."

"Yeah, that's one of those hard things to walk back on."

"You ever cheat on your wife?"

"No," Carter said. "But I think she thought my job was cheating enough." Carter studied Brandon's face to see if he understood. But when it didn't appear that his buddy did, he explained, "She always said that the navy was my mistress, and I didn't need a wife."

"Ah," Brandon said. "Ain't that a bitch. You always wanted to go into the navy. Me? I just wanted to ride horses. And you? Well, you were out there, searching after every bloody naval experience you could get your hands on."

"I sure was," Carter added. "And still would be if it didn't mean riding a desk. That's not for me."

"Not to mention the time period you were off on discharge, right?"

"Medical was pretty rough," he said. "Lots of surgeries but I'm good now."

"Are you?" Carter knew he was asking so much more than about surgeries.

"Yeah," he said. "I am. I'm sorry for not coming home earlier, but sometimes …"

"I know. … I know after my dad died, I kind of went AWOL for a time. I walked away from everybody. I didn't know how to handle it. Took me about a year and a half before I slowly got back to normal."

"Exactly," Carter said. "Life can sometimes send you in a tizzy, and you don't know if you're coming or going."

"I hear you. And, speaking of which, I have to stop at a couple places and pick up stuff. You know the drill."

"Yep. Never make two trips if you could make it all happen in one."

Brandon chuckled. "Exactly. Got to go to the feed store, hit the vet's, God only knows what else."

"At the vet's, I'll come in and ask about the dog," Carter said. "I know this one's a long shot. But I said I'd check it out."

"What do you mean by *this one*?" Brandon asked curiously.

Carter explained about the K9 program that was now defunct in the military and the request to the Titanium Corp that he'd been working with.

"Wow. So Uncle Sam really wants to know about this dog?"

"They'd like to know as long as it doesn't cost man-hours and money," Carter said in a dry tone. "I'm not getting paid to do this. This is a good-heart mission."

"We all need those," Brandon said. "Hell, I had lambs in the house for six weeks this spring because winter hit so bad."

"How many?"

"Twelve," he said in disgust. "And we always have a calf or two. But, boy, this year the house got pretty darn crowded."

"I bet Debbie didn't complain."

"Nope, she didn't. She was in her element."

"Still no children, huh?"

Brandon shook his head, and his face looked drawn and tired. "No. Not likely to be any. That's the rest of the issue between us."

"Did you ever get tested?"

"Nah. I didn't bother. Either it would happen or it won't."

"That's not necessarily good enough for Debbie," Carter said. "I know for a fact she wanted a big family."

"But putting the money into that IVF stuff? Jeez, that's expensive. And no guarantees."

"No, but if you don't go and get tested, they can't tell what the problem is either."

"So Debbie told me," Brandon said in a note of gloom. "Something else I screwed up."

At that, Carter had to laugh. They pulled up at the feed store, hopped out and wandered around. A scene that was fondly remembered from all the holidays and weekends he'd spent here with his buddy. They quickly loaded up the supplies and headed on down the street to the vet's.

While Brandon got the medicine he needed, Carter talked to a couple of the women at the front about the missing dog. "Matzuka is his name," he said. "He's a huge shepherd-cross and was part of the War Dogs Department. He was flown here for an adoptive family. They said they never got him."

The nurse frowned and asked, "Who was the family?"

"Longfellow." His voice was hesitant as he pulled his notes from his pocket to double-check.

Only silence came from the women.

He glanced up and asked, "Problems?"

They both hesitated.

"I am here at the official request of Commander Cross of the US Navy. That dog gave a lot of years of service to our country. He deserves to have a comfortable life of retirement."

"It would be hard to imagine that family would have been given the dog," she said. "They're pretty rough on them."

"Rough in what way?"

"There have been complaints about their treatment of animals."

"Okay. So are we thinking they may have gotten the dog and then hurt him?"

"We're not saying anything," the receptionist said. She glanced at the other one and said, "We don't know anything."

"Do you know where this family lives?"

"Yep," the second woman said. She picked up a piece of paper and drew a map. "Here." She handed it to him.

"Any way to contact them?"

They just shook their heads.

Carter nodded. "I can get that from the government. Thanks very much." He turned and walked outside, studying the map. One of the things he would have to do pretty damn fast was get a set of wheels. Of his own. Although Brandon had several ranch trucks, Carter wasn't sure how much traveling he would have to do for this mission, and he'd feel better if he paid his own way. Although Brandon would smack him hard for saying that.

As he stood here, Brandon popped out and asked, "Ready to go?"

They hopped into the vehicle and headed toward the ranch. "Any idea who the Longfellow family are?"

"Shysters," Brandon said succinctly. "Not the kind of folks you want to hang around with. But wealthy business people for the most part. Pioneers of the town and they own most of it."

"That's the family this dog was supposed to be adopted out to."

"If they had the dog, and they say they didn't, chances are they've already shot it and buried it."

"I hope not," Carter said, "because I'll be mighty pissed if that's the case."

"And why's that?"

"Because the dog lost a leg, like I did. Because the dog served his country, like I also gave a lot of time and effort to my country. Last thing I want is to think somebody would take me out and shoot me because I'm *useless*."

"You never gave us that chance," Brandon said calmly. "You took yourself out of this world all on your own. I didn't have a chance to tell you that I didn't give a shit if you had one leg or no legs. But you wouldn't even give me that opportunity."

Carter laughed. "Good point. Very good point." As they drove down the long driveway to the main house, he asked the question he'd been holding back on. "How is Haley these days?"

"Pretty mad, as usual," Brandon said happily.

"If you wouldn't pick on her so much," Carter said, "she wouldn't always be upset with you."

"But it brings me joy," Brandon said. "Besides, that's what brothers are for."

"That's what brothers are for when you're kids. Hardly what brothers are for at your age."

"Thirty-two is not old, and she just turned thirty, and I'm not letting her forget it."

"Ouch," Carter said. "Unless she's married with her two-point-three kids, she won't take that reminder well."

"No, she doesn't," he said smugly. "She's not married."

"Oh, I'm sorry for her then. I know having a family was a huge dream for her."

"I figure she's waiting for you to come back."

"Why the hell would you think that?" Carter demanded. "All we ever did was fight."

"What's wrong with fighting? I think all these calm, boring relationships are overrated."

"Yeah, but not everybody wants to argue about everything in life either."

"Well, she doesn't know you're coming."

"That's probably not fair. She doesn't like me."

"She can deal with it," Brandon said. "I told her that I'd get you back here somehow."

Carter laughed. "You haven't changed a bit."

"Nope, I haven't. Don't you forget that."

"How can I possibly?" They pulled up to the front of the

main house, and Carter sat here for a long moment, staring at it. "I have a lot of really good memories here. I'm so sorry about your dad."

"Me too," Brandon said. "The fact that he died around the same time you had your accident just made it that much harder. You couldn't come for the funeral, and I couldn't come to your side. Once he passed on, there was nobody else to handle the ranch."

"Being at my side wouldn't help anybody," Carter said. "I don't blame you, and I wouldn't have wanted you there anyway. I was a mess. I was in pieces, literally and figuratively."

Brandon winced. "Come on in. Let's put on some coffee. And I've got to tell you how it's damn fine to have you home." The two guys exited the truck, heading for the house.

Just then the side door slammed open and out stalked Haley—tall, her red hair in a braid down the center of her back. She was dressed in jeans with work boots and a plaid shirt. She was the epitome of a cowgirl.

But Carter also knew she was an incredibly talented financial analyst and was a partner in an investment company in town where she worked. She lived at the ranch with her brother. Always had. She'd planned to build a second house for herself but hadn't gotten that far yet. At least he assumed so when he saw her coming outside from the side door in the kitchen.

She was glaring at Brandon when her gaze switched over to Carter. He waited for the moment of recognition to slam into her, and then her face went white. But, instead of saying something which he could give a snappy comeback to, her gaze went up one side and down the other; then she spun on her heels and walked back inside.

His heart dropped like a stone. He looked over at his buddy and said, "I told you that I shouldn't have come back."

"Not only should you have come back," Brandon said, anger threading through his voice, "you are very, *very* welcome to be here. Regardless of what she has to say."

This concludes Book 6 of The K9 Files: Parker.

Read about Carter: The K9 Files, Book 7

THE K9 FILES: CARTER (BOOK #7)

Welcome to the all new K9 Files series reconnecting readers with the unforgettable men from SEALs of Steel in a new series of action packed, page turning romantic suspense that fans have come to expect from USA TODAY Bestselling author Dale Mayer. Pssst... you'll meet other favorite characters from SEALs of Honor and Heroes for Hire too!

Staying away was harder than he thought ...

Recovering from an accident was hell on anyone, but, for a stubborn guy like Carter, it was worse. No way would he be a burden. So he stayed away from Montana, where his best friend lived ... and his best friend's sister.

Until Geir and Cade ask Carter to check up on a dog delivered to a small town close by, but the dog never arrived. Considering this was one of the missing War Dogs that Titanium Corp was handling, Carter was happy to assist. Maybe even relieved as it gave him a reason to go where he'd been afraid to go before.

Walking into her partner's office to find his dead body on the floor had sent Hailey down a nightmarish path that never seemed to end. Then it *had* started with Carter's arrival. What else should she expect from the man who she'd always loved and who had rejected her time and time again. She'd hoped the attraction to him would have lessened by now, but it was even worse.

As the body count mounts, and the town takes sides, Hailey realizes that Carter was always the one to back her up, even when it meant he could die in this fight that's gone to hell. Particularly when Carter finds the missing K9 dog, and his current owner is on the wrong side of the war ...

Only Carter doesn't care, knowing he'd always stand on the side of right, but *maybe*—if he was lucky this time—he wouldn't be standing alone ...

Find Book 7 here!
To find out more visit Dale Mayer's website.
http://smarturl.it/DMSCarter

Author's Note

Thank you for reading Parker: The K9 Files, Book 6! If you enjoyed the book, please take a moment and leave a short review.

Dear reader,

I love to hear from readers, and you can contact me at my website: www.dalemayer.com or at my Facebook author page. To be informed of new releases and special offers, sign up for my newsletter or follow me on BookBub. And if you are interested in joining Dale Mayer's Reader Group, here is the Facebook sign up page.
https://smarturl.it/DaleMayerFBGroup

Cheers,
Dale Mayer

Get THREE Free Books Now!

Have you met the SEALS of Honor?

SEALs of Honor Books 1, 2, and 3. Follow the stories of brave, badass warriors who serve their country with honor and love their women to the limits of life and death.

Read Mason, Hawk, and Dane right now for FREE.

Go here and tell me where to send them!
http://smarturl.it/EthanBofB

About the Author

Dale Mayer is a USA Today bestselling author best known for her Psychic Visions and Family Blood Ties series. Her contemporary romances are raw and full of passion and emotion (Second Chances, SKIN), her thrillers will keep you guessing (By Death series), and her romantic comedies will keep you giggling (It's a Dog's Life and Charmin Marvin Romantic Comedy series).

She honors the stories that come to her – and some of them are crazy and break all the rules and cross multiple genres!

To go with her fiction, she also writes nonfiction in many different fields with books available on resume writing, companion gardening and the US mortgage system. She has recently published her Career Essentials Series. All her books are available in print and ebook format.

Connect with Dale Mayer Online

Dale's Website – www.dalemayer.com
Facebook Personal – https://smarturl.it/DaleMayer
Instagram – https://smarturl.it/DaleMayerInstagram
BookBub – https://smarturl.it/DaleMayerBookbub
Facebook Fan Page – https://smarturl.it/DaleMayerFBFanPage
Goodreads – https://smarturl.it/DaleMayerGoodreads

Also by Dale Mayer

Published Adult Books:

Hathaway House

Aaron, Book 1

Brock, Book 2

Cole, Book 3

Denton, Book 4

Elliot, Book 5

Finn, Book 6

Gregory, Book 7

Heath, Book 8

The K9 Files

Ethan, Book 1

Pierce, Book 2

Zane, Book 3

Blaze, Book 4

Lucas, Book 5

Parker, Book 6

Carter, Book 7

Lovely Lethal Gardens

Arsenic in the Azaleas, Book 1

Bones in the Begonias, Book 2

Corpse in the Carnations, Book 3

Daggers in the Dahlias, Book 4

Evidence in the Echinacea, Book 5
Footprints in the Ferns, Book 6
Gun in the Gardenias, Book 7
Handcuffs in the Heather, Book 8

Psychic Vision Series
Tuesday's Child
Hide 'n Go Seek
Maddy's Floor
Garden of Sorrow
Knock Knock...
Rare Find
Eyes to the Soul
Now You See Her
Shattered
Into the Abyss
Seeds of Malice
Eye of the Falcon
Itsy-Bitsy Spider
Unmasked
Deep Beneath
From the Ashes
Psychic Visions Books 1–3
Psychic Visions Books 4–6
Psychic Visions Books 7–9

By Death Series
Touched by Death
Haunted by Death
Chilled by Death
By Death Books 1–3

Broken Protocols – Romantic Comedy Series

Cat's Meow
Cat's Pajamas
Cat's Cradle
Cat's Claus
Broken Protocols 1-4

Broken and... Mending

Skin
Scars
Scales (of Justice)
Broken but... Mending 1-3

Glory

Genesis
Tori
Celeste
Glory Trilogy

Biker Blues

Morgan: Biker Blues, Volume 1
Cash: Biker Blues, Volume 2

SEALs of Honor

Mason: SEALs of Honor, Book 1
Hawk: SEALs of Honor, Book 2
Dane: SEALs of Honor, Book 3
Swede: SEALs of Honor, Book 4
Shadow: SEALs of Honor, Book 5
Cooper: SEALs of Honor, Book 6
Markus: SEALs of Honor, Book 7
Evan: SEALs of Honor, Book 8

Mason's Wish: SEALs of Honor, Book 9

Chase: SEALs of Honor, Book 10

Brett: SEALs of Honor, Book 11

Devlin: SEALs of Honor, Book 12

Easton: SEALs of Honor, Book 13

Ryder: SEALs of Honor, Book 14

Macklin: SEALs of Honor, Book 15

Corey: SEALs of Honor, Book 16

Warrick: SEALs of Honor, Book 17

Tanner: SEALs of Honor, Book 18

Jackson: SEALs of Honor, Book 19

Kanen: SEALs of Honor, Book 20

Nelson: SEALs of Honor, Book 21

Taylor: SEALs of Honor, Book 22

Colton: SEALs of Honor, Book 23

SEALs of Honor, Books 1–3

SEALs of Honor, Books 4–6

SEALs of Honor, Books 7–10

SEALs of Honor, Books 11–13

SEALs of Honor, Books 14–16

SEALs of Honor, Books 17–19

Heroes for Hire

Levi's Legend: Heroes for Hire, Book 1

Stone's Surrender: Heroes for Hire, Book 2

Merk's Mistake: Heroes for Hire, Book 3

Rhodes's Reward: Heroes for Hire, Book 4

Flynn's Firecracker: Heroes for Hire, Book 5

Logan's Light: Heroes for Hire, Book 6

Harrison's Heart: Heroes for Hire, Book 7

Saul's Sweetheart: Heroes for Hire, Book 8

Dakota's Delight: Heroes for Hire, Book 9

SEALs of Steel

The Mavericks
Kerrick, Book 1
Griffin, Book 2
Jax, Book 3
Beau, Book 4
Asher, Book 5
Ryker, Book 6
Miles, Book 7
Nico, Book 8
Keane, Book 9
Lennox, Book 10
Gavin, Book 11
Shane, Book 12

Collections
Dare to Be You…
Dare to Love…
Dare to be Strong…
RomanceX3

Standalone Novellas
It's a Dog's Life
Riana's Revenge
Second Chances

Published Young Adult Books:

Family Blood Ties Series
Vampire in Denial
Vampire in Distress
Vampire in Design
Vampire in Deceit

Vampire in Defiance
Vampire in Conflict
Vampire in Chaos
Vampire in Crisis
Vampire in Control
Vampire in Charge
Family Blood Ties Set 1–3
Family Blood Ties Set 1–5
Family Blood Ties Set 4–6
Family Blood Ties Set 7–9
Sian's Solution, A Family Blood Ties Series Prequel
    Novelette

Design series
Dangerous Designs
Deadly Designs
Darkest Designs
Design Series Trilogy

Standalone
In Cassie's Corner
Gem Stone (a Gemma Stone Mystery)
Time Thieves

Published Non-Fiction Books:

Career Essentials
Career Essentials: The Résumé
Career Essentials: The Cover Letter
Career Essentials: The Interview
Career Essentials: 3 in 1

Printed in Poland
by Amazon Fulfillment
Poland Sp. z o.o., Wrocław

57583436R00123